JACK MARTIN

THE MAN FROM JERUSALEM

Complete and Unabridged

LINFORD
Leicester

First published in Great Britain in 2015 by
Robert Hale Limited
London

First Linford Edition
published 2018
by arrangement with
Robert Hale
an imprint of
The Crowood Press
Wiltshire

A catalogue record for this book is available
from the British Library.

ISBN 978–1–4448–3630–1

Published by
F. A. Thorpe (Publishing)
Anstey, Leicestershire

Set by Words & Graphics Ltd.
Anstey, Leicestershire
Printed and bound in Great Britain by
T. J. International Ltd., Padstow, Cornwall

This book is printed on acid-free paper

This one is for Georgia
and offered with love and affection

THE MAN FROM JERUSALEM

Day after day, the sun does its utmost to roast the very land upon which the dilapidated town of Jerusalem sits. Johnny Jerusalem is returning home to the town of his namesake. He'd left years ago, but no sooner is he back than the little money he has is stolen from him during a bank robbery. He sets out with a young gunslinger to find the culprits who have wronged him — but there's a posse behind them, and bandits ahead of them, and soon the bullets are flying . . .

Books by Jack Martin
in the Linford Western Library:

THE TARNISHED STAR
ARKANSAS SMITH
THE BALLAD OF DELTA ROSE
WILD BILL WILLIAMS
THE AFTERLIFE OF SLIM McCORD

Prologue

'You're free to go,' the lawman said and handed over Johnny's guns, billfold and pocketknife.

Johnny placed his gun belt on and pushed his billfold into his pocket. He dropped the knife into another pocket.

'You do best to be leaving town,' the lawman advised, staring at Johnny through pale green eyes. It was difficult to read the lawman's expression beneath the thick shaggy beard he wore.

'I'll be on the next train,' Johnny said. He had just enough money in his billfold to get him to where he wanted to be.

'And I'd advise against coming back.'

'Don't worry,' Johnny said and turned for the door. 'I won't be coming back.'

Prologue

1

'Jerusalem,' yelled the conductor. 'End of the line.'

End of the line, Johnny Jerusalem smiled at that. 'Sure got that right,' he mumbled as he made his way along the small boxcar and stepped out into the harsh afternoon sunshine. The now stationary train seemed to pant like a horse that had been ridden far too hard for far too many miles; a black plume spluttered from its smokestack and hung motionless in an otherwise featureless sky.

'Good to be home,' Johnny said with a tight grin and took the makings from his shirt pocket. He quickly put together a quirly and, carrying only a small carpetbag, crossed the station and headed towards the centre of the town for which he was named. The town looked much the same to him but then

3

nothing much changed around Jerusalem.

The town of Jerusalem had been founded in 1825 by a band of wandering Christians looking to claim a part of the West for their order. First they had built a church, and then as the membership grew a town was erected around it. Gradually the town had grown into a vibrant, if over-pious community, but with the turning of the years the population had dwindled and folk had gone off in search of better lives elsewhere. There wasn't really very much to keep folks in Jerusalem, though some stayed just as some would always stay, feeling that the town, for all its faults, was home and was where they belonged. There were times when it seemed that even the Good Lord above might have had something personal against the town of Jerusalem, for day after day, except during wintertime when the snow and rain were thrown at a person, the sun did its utmost to roast the very land upon which the dilapidated town sat. And if the almost constant heat wasn't enough to make the fools who lived there miserable, then there was the wind, a scorching breeze, which blew in across the flats and dried the spittle on a man's lips and the tears in his eyes. There were always a lot of red weary eyes in Jerusalem.

Johnny Jerusalem had been born here, or at least he thought that was the case. All he really knew for certain was that he had been found here, a newborn infant wrapped in a dirty old horse-blanket and left screaming in the main street. That had been almost thirty-five years ago and although he couldn't recall anything of the day that he had been discovered, a little old baby just about holding on to life, he knew the events perfectly well. He had been told them often enough.

'Johnny Jerusalem. That sure is a face from the past.'

The words broke Johnny's train of thought and he looked up and straight into the face of Hoss Banson. He looked just as Johnny had remembered him, perhaps a little heavier but just as mean and surly. The thing that truly took Johnny by surprise about the man was that Hoss was wearing the badge of the sheriff's office. It was pinned to his shirtfront and the sun caught it in such a way that Johnny had to shield his eyes against the glare.

'What fool went and made you sheriff?' Johnny asked, smiling to sugar the remark.

'Don't you worry none about that,' Hoss said. 'Question is what brings you back to Jerusalem? I figured this town weren't vibrant enough for a big shot like Johnny Jerusalem.'

'I ain't no big shot.'

The sheriff ran a hand over the stubble on his chin. 'All the same,' he said, 'I never thought I'd see you coming back here.'

'It's home,' Johnny said, simply.

'You've been away a long time.'

'I have,' Johnny agreed.

A tight smile drew across the sheriff's face. 'Like I say you've been gone a long time,' he said. 'You'll find things have changed around here.'

'Well I see the sheriff's sure changed,' Johnny said. 'What happened to Deke Carter?'

'He died.'

'Just died?'

'Hunting accident,' Hoss said. 'Fell from his horse, snapped his leg and gangrene set in. Damn fool wouldn't let the doc take his leg, said he'd come into this world with two legs and intended on going out just the same. Said he weren't going to hobble into the afterlife like some damn cripple but walk through those pearly gates with all his limbs intact.'

'Guess he got his wish,' Johnny said, sardonically.

Hoss nodded and pulled a slim cigar from his breast pocket. He struck a match on the heel of a boot and sucked the smoke to life.

'The gangrene killed the stubborn old fool,' he said. 'If he'd let the saw-bones take the leg he'd likely be here now, a one-legged man sure enough but living all the same. As it is now he may have two legs but none are doing him any good beneath the ground.'

'Too bad,' Johnny said. He'd liked Deke Carter, had always found him to be a fair and honourable man. He'd done a good job of lawing the small town and although he could display a firm hand when it was needed he would usually smooth out trouble before it really started. Which, given what Johnny knew, would likely be the opposite of the way Hoss would do things. Hoss had always been a braggart and a bully. The type of man who pushed his weight around a little too much, made his opinions too well known. He was the last man you'd expect to see wearing the tin star.

'Still, he went on his own terms,' Hoss said. 'There's something to be said for that.'

'I guess so,' Johnny spat on to the ground. 'Poor old Deke.'

'Yeah,' Hoss smiled. 'Poor old Deke.'

For several moments silence fell between the two men. They stood there, facing each other, looking directly into each other's eyes. It was Johnny who looked away first. He had history with Hoss Banson and none of it was any good, but he'd be dammed if he was going to let the fact that Banson was town sheriff bother him none. He looked up and down the street, though saw nothing in particular, and then shook his head. It surely looked as if Jerusalem, the town, was down on its luck. Just like Jerusalem, the man, really.

'And now you're the sheriff,' Johnny said. Well, the man had two good legs. He had to give him that.

Hoss allowed an elongated stream of creamy-looking smoke to escape between his teeth.

'Going on for four years now,' he said. 'I keep a quiet town. That's the way folks like it around here.'

Now it was Johnny's turn to smile.

'Seems quiet enough for me,' he said and pushed past the man. 'Be seeing you, Hoss.'

'Oh I'm sure of it,' the sheriff said, speaking to Johnny's back. 'I'm mighty sure of it.'

2

Johnny decided to call in at the Indian Creek Saloon and maybe get a drink to wash some of the dust from his throat. The saloon had been named for the creek that ran down from the mountains and skirted the town before flowing into the river that was often so low that the stones upon its bed were dry surface side up.

A stiff drink is just the thing, Johnny told himself. Yeah he'd allow himself one before going on to the ranch house he'd been left in old Walt's last will and testament. The ranch had been unoccupied for some time and it was likely he had a lot of work ahead of him so he wouldn't begrudge himself a drink. Just the one, though, he told himself. Knowing that too often it had been drink that had led him merrily into all sorts of trouble. It was the drink and the crazy schemes that always seemed so dandy when viewed from within an alcohol haze that had kept Johnny away from the town for so long. These days Johnny wasn't really a drinking man and he intended to keep it that way, but just the one wouldn't do him no ill.

Johnny had been working in Reno when he'd received word that Walt Bren, the man who had been the closest thing he'd ever had to a pa, had died. The news had come by telegram and even then Johnny hadn't come straight back to Jerusalem, but had instead drunk away the wages he'd made as a ranch-hand and spent fourteen days in the Reno Jailhouse after belting a town official in the mouth following a drunken argument. When Johnny had been released he'd spent another month doing back-breaking work in order to earn enough money for the journey back to Jerusalem.

The telegram had explained that Johnny had an inheritance coming to him. The old man had no real blood kin and so he'd left everything he owned, which amounted to little more than a rundown ranch, to Johnny. There was also a meagre amount of money but once the legal fees were deducted and expenses covered Johnny figured he'd receive maybe enough to buy himself a meal. None of that really mattered to Johnny though, since he'd never had any real money, and it was difficult to miss what he'd never really had. Any monies willed to him didn't matter at all but the fact that the old man had gone . . . well, that mattered. That was all that mattered. Walt Bren had raised Johnny as if he had been his own son and Johnny figured that he already owed more to the old man than he could ever have repaid. And even now, in death, the old man was looking out for Johnny, giving him a home, somewhere to call his own.

Of course when Johnny had left Jerusalem five years back he had intended to return with a fortune made and pay back the old man for all he had done for him, give him some security in his dotage. Life, however, had not turned out as expected for Johnny Jerusalem, it never did, and he'd returned to town with less in his pockets than he'd started out with. Hell, he didn't even own a horse.

The saloon was quiet and Johnny made his way directly to the counter and ordered himself a cold beer. The barkeep, a balding man whom Johnny didn't recognize, quickly placed a foaming glass in front of him and held out his hand for payment. Johnny filled the hand with a coin and took a sip of the beer. It tasted mighty good as it went down his parched throat.

'I could do with something to eat,' Johnny said, taking another sip of the beer.

'I could get my wife to fry you up some eggs, bacon and beans,' the barkeep said.

'Thanks,' Johnny said and drained his beer. He handed the glass back to the barkeep, asked for another and paid for both the drinks and the meal.

'Sit yourself down,' the barkeep said. 'I'll bring your food over when it's ready.'

'Obliged,' Johnny said and went and selected a corner table with a good view of the batwings — that way he could see who came in. He felt a little guilty at having a second beer but he figured that as long as he stayed off the whiskey he'd be fine. Now that he was back in his hometown he was starting to feel a little nostalgic and he wondered if any familiar faces would push through the batwings in search of subsistence. At the moment there were only three other men in the saloon and Johnny knew none of them. None of the faces in the saloon had been here five years ago and Johnny figured that he was the one who was truly the stranger.

He drained his drink, went back to the counter and ordered yet another, thinking this was definitely the last one. The barkeep handed him his food at the same time. It smelt delicious and

14

Johnny felt his stomach do a cartwheel. The barkeep handed him a fork and knife.

'Once again I'm obliged,' Johnny said. He was about to go back to his corner table when he saw a familiar face come through the batwings. Johnny smiled warmly and looked at the old-timer, who caught his eye and then smiled himself.

'Can I buy you a drink?' Johnny asked.

'Well thank you kindly,' Jessie Walker said and smiled, revealing that he had lost damn near all his teeth in the years since Johnny had seen him last. He had a single chopper each side of his mouth and they looked like fangs when he smiled. 'Sure is nice to see you back in Jerusalem.'

Johnny ordered a beer for the old man and led him over to the corner table where both men sat down.

'When'd you get back?' the old man asked, taking a long sip of his beer. He smacked his lips and immediately took another sip.

'Got in on the noon train,' Johnny

said, chewing on a mouthful of bacon.

'I was mighty sorry when your pa died,' the old man said. 'He was a good man.'

Johnny smiled, swallowed audibly.

'He weren't exactly my pa,' he said, 'but yeah, he was a good man. The best kind of man.'

'Not your pa.' The old man gave his vampiric smile. 'He was the only pa you ever knew.'

'That's true,' Johnny mumbled through a mouthful of beans.

'Is it that your pa died brought you back here?' The old man took another sip of his beer. 'After all this time, I mean?'

'I meant to come back sooner,' Johnny said, aware that he sounded defensive but there was nothing he could do about that. If truth were told there was a guilt burning deep down in his stomach over the fact that he'd been away so long, that he had not returned to see the man who had loved him like a son, raised him as if he had been his own. 'But I kept putting it off, hoping

16

that I'd strike lucky in the next town down the road and be able to return a successful man.'

The old man nodded his understanding.

'But that never happened?' he asked.

'No.' Johnny shook his head. He scooped up the last of the beans with his fork, chewed them and swallowed. 'I've been drifting mostly, taking whatever jobs I could find. I've been everything from a ranch-hand to a gambler to a lawman. I've done it all, bounty hunting, Indian fighting; I even tried gold prospecting a few years back but nothing panned out the way I hoped.'

The old man nodded, knowingly. He said nothing in reply and instead took another sip of his beer.

'Seems I left it a little too late to come back,' Johnny said. 'I'd sure have liked to see old Walt again but I guess it's too late now.'

'You're here now,' the old man said. 'That's what really matters.'

For a moment there was silence

between the two men. Both were lost in their own thoughts and it was the old man who finally broke the silence.

'So what are your plans for the old place?' he asked. 'I suppose you'll be wanting to sell up and move on again?'

'Hell no.' Johnny drained his beer. 'Figured I've seen enough of everywhere else and I'm just about ready to settle back here. I figure I'll work the old ranch, build it up.'

'That old place is pretty run down,' the old man said. 'Your pa did his best but he hadn't been a well man this last year or so.'

Johnny had a piece of bacon trapped between his teeth and he worried at it with his tongue. 'I need to get the ranch working again,' he said. 'See if I can't turn it into something worthwhile. Turn it into something good, which seems the best way to honour Walt's memory. I think he would have liked that, to see the old place prospering.'

'That's good,' the old man said and drained his own beer. 'Walt sure would

18

have liked that.'

'Another?' Johnny asked holding up his empty beer glass. The resolution he'd made to only have the one drink had clearly been forgotten.

'Sure thing,' the old man said and took the glass from Johnny. 'But this time I'm buying.'

Johnny, who had little money in his pockets, was not going to argue with that.

The two men spent the afternoon drinking and they'd both consumed a sizeable amount of the cold beer by the time they left the saloon and stepped out into the dying afternoon sun. They were both a little unsteady on their feet and the old man had to hold on to Johnny to save himself from falling face down in the dirt.

'How you getting out to the ranch?' the old man asked, breathing beer fumes as he spoke.

'Guess I'm walking,' Johnny said. 'A good walk will help to clear my head in any case.'

'Walking,' the old man spat. 'What are you? Some kind of transient?'

'Guess that ain't far from the truth,' Johnny said.

'I can loan you a horse,' the old man said. 'Let's go back to my place and saddle you up.'

'Obliged,' Johnny said and then he saw yet another familiar face coming down the street towards them. It was a woman and although he hadn't seen her in many years he instantly recognized her as Cherry Mewis. She was just as bonny as he'd remembered. She'd be in her mid-thirties now but looked at least five years younger. The passing of time had done little to tarnish her beauty. She'd always had the most striking eyes and now as the sun glinted off them Johnny felt a stirring of memory that made him feel awkward.

'Howdy, Miss Mewis,' the old man said as the woman drew level with them.

She smiled and then a slight frown crossed her face. 'Are you drunk, Mr Walker.' It wasn't a question. 'This time of the day you should be ashamed of yourself.'

'I'm celebrating,' the old man said and slapped Johnny on the back. 'Ain't everyday you bump into an old friend.'

The woman looked at Johnny and at first she couldn't seem to place him but then recognition dawned in her eyes. For the briefest of moments a smile seemed to register on her face but it was quickly replaced by a stern look.

'Johnny,' she said. 'Johnny Jerusalem?'

'Nice to see you, Miss Mewis,' Johnny said and hoped she couldn't smell the beer on his own breath. 'It's been a long time.'

'A long time,' she said.

'Longer than I would have liked,' Johnny admitted. For the briefest of moments he remembered her as she was the last time he had been in town. He also recalled how things had been between them but he chased the memories away. What's done was done.

The woman smiled, gave a slight nod and then looked up the street as though looking out for someone. She adjusted her bonnet and seemed to flush slightly as though embarrassed.

'I was sorry to hear about your father,' she said.

Johnny nodded, smiled slightly.

'I thank you for your sympathy,' he said.

'Old Walt was well thought of,' the old man put in.

'Seems that way,' Johnny said.

'He was a good man,' Cherry said. 'Everyone liked him.'

For a moment there was silence, during which time Johnny felt his stomach churning and he had to bite back the bile in his throat. He took a deep breath, fearing he was going to be sick, which just wouldn't do in front of the woman. Just wouldn't do at all.

'Well, if you gentlemen will excuse me,' the woman said, herself feeling awkward. 'I've got errands to run.'

'Sure thing, Miss Mewis,' Johnny said. 'Sure is nice to see you again, though.'

Once again the woman smiled. It was a polite smile rather than a warm one and seemed tinged with regret. She then made her way back down the street.

For several moments the two men watched her go but then the old man hawked up a lump from his throat and spat it into the dirt.

'If I was a young fella like you I'd be chasing after her,' he said.

'I'm too drunk to walk properly,' Johnny said, 'let alone chase after a bonny young lady.'

'I'd chase her all the same.' The old man spat into the street. 'It's been my experience that they sometimes don't run all that fast.'

'Maybe,' Johnny said. 'But I reckon it would be too fast for me.'

'I'm the old man,' Jessie said. 'Not you. I'd trade places with you at the drop of a hat. Hell if I could shed just ten of these years I'm carrying, why I'd be down that street like a pure-bred racehorse.'

Johnny smiled, thinking that there

had been a time when he'd felt something romantic could have developed between himself and Cherry Mewis, but that had been a long time ago and seemed now to have been a part of another life.

'You mentioned loaning me a horse,' he said, quickly changing the subject but keeping his gaze on Cherry Mewis for a moment longer.

The old man grinned.

'That I did,' he said. 'That I did.'

3

Johnny pulled on the Appaloosa's reins and held the beast steady. He looked down into the valley. There below him was the ranch he had inherited. For several moments he stared at it, remembering the good times he'd spent there.

In the evening light it had something of an ethereal quality about it; the way the fading light danced across the ground gave the place an almost ghostly pallor.

It had been Walt who had come across Johnny in the streets of Jerusalem and brought him here to the ranch where his wife Elisa had taken one look at the baby, by all accounts close to death, and taken him into the house where she had nursed him back to health. Of course the town's sheriff had started a search for the baby's folks but as the weeks went by, turned into months, and then a year it became clear that whoever the baby's true folks were they weren't going to come forward and were most likely far away from the town of Jerusalem. The theory was, so Johnny had been told, that his real folks had left him in the town in the hope that someone would come across him, take care of him and raise him as their own. Maybe his real ma and pa, whoever they were, couldn't care for him for whatever reason and had figured that by leaving him in town he had a fighting chance of survival. During that period there was a lot of drifting going on, a lot of families moving out West in search of some kind of promised land on the prairies, among the plains or in the mountains. Few of them ever found it and most discovered that the reality was a hell of a lot harder than they'd ever imagined.

Elisa and Walt had named the baby Johnny and rather than giving him their own surname they had given him the town's name. It made sense, Walt had told Johnny years later, since they figured that one day his real folks would turn up and lay claim to him. That never happened and the identity of Johnny's folks remained a mystery. Not that Johnny cared since he'd had a good life with Walt and Elisa and had long since stopped wondering about his real parents.

Johnny was just shy of ten years old when Elisa passed away and the loss had hit the young boy like a sledgehammer. She'd been the only mother he had ever known and even now, all these years later, Johnny still missed the woman. From the day she passed Walt had taken over the role of both mother and father, and under his guidance Johnny had grown into a fine, if restless, young man.

Johnny spurred the horse forward, carefully negotiating the incline down to the valley floor and towards the house. He felt a little unsteady in the saddle, no doubt a result of all the beer he'd consumed, and he had to grip the reins tightly as he felt his stomach turn.

'Good thing you're sober,' Johnny said, patting his horse. The beast ignored him and continued its careful path down the hill.

Eventually Johnny reached the valley floor and although his stomach was still churning — being bounced about in the saddle wasn't helping none — he did feel a little better. It wasn't far off dark and he figured that he'd bed down for the night and take stock come morning. He spurred the horse into a semi gallop, which once again made him feel nauseous, but nevertheless he kept up the pace and within moments he had reached the ranch house and was able to dismount.

'Home sweet home,' Johnny said as he tethered the horse to the hitching rail. He thought about putting the horse into the barn for the night but it was a mild evening and he figured it would do just fine tethered outside. He didn't even remove the saddle but took his rifle from the boot. Then on unsteady feet his made his way towards the front door.

Johnny turned the handle and then pushed the door. It responded with a slight creek but opened easily enough. The door could be locked from the inside using a post which slid through two steel latches, but old Walt had never seen the need to fit proper locks to the door. Using his sleeve Johnny mopped sweat from his brow and stepped into the gloomy interior of the house. It was in that moment that he seemed to sober up immediately and he worked the lever on his rifle and held it up in aim.

'Who the hell are you?' Johnny asked, levelling the rifle at the young man who had been asleep on the cot and obviously hadn't heard Johnny approach.

'Don't shoot, mister,' the man who was little more than a kid said and sat up, holding his hands above his head. Johnny noticed that the man wore no gun belt and didn't appear to be armed. He seemed to be as startled as Johnny was himself.

'I repeat,' Johnny said. 'Who the hell are you?'

'My name's Wyatt,' the young man said. 'Wyatt Everett and I don't mean no harm.'

'What you doing here?'

'I was sleeping,' the young man said with a slight smile, though that much had been obvious. 'I didn't figure anyone lived here and thought the place abandoned. I kinda been living here.'

Johnny noticed the young man's gun belt on the wooden table beside the cot and he crossed the room and reached out for it. He tossed the rig into the far corner and then lowered his own weapon.

'Living here? How long?'

The kid shrugged his shoulders.

'A few weeks,' he said.

'A few weeks?'

'Yeah, maybe a month. That's why I figured the place was abandoned. It didn't look like anyone had been in here for a long while; there was a thick coat of dust over everything. I had to clean the place up some. I fixed your stove, mister.'

Johnny looked around and the place sure did look spick and span.

'So you figured on moving in and claiming the place for yourself?'

'Yeah.' The young man shook his head. 'I mean no. Look, mister I don't want no trouble. I just figured I'd stay here for a short time and see if anyone turned up. I had nowhere else to go and I didn't figure I was doing any harm. I would have moved on when the mood took me. I mean I was always going to move on sooner or later.'

'So where's home for you?' Johnny sat himself down on the small wooden chair beside the fireplace and took his makings from his pocket. He rolled himself a smoke and tossed his makings to Wyatt, who was, by now, sitting on the edge of the cot.

'Obliged.' The young man quickly put a smoke together. 'I don't suppose I got one. A home, that is. I've been working up and down the country. Mostly cows, signing myself on to whatever outfit were looking for men and then moving on when the job ended. I kind of drifted here and with winter coming I thought I'd stick around but I never intended no disrespect. No sir, the last thing I intended was any disrespect.'

Johnny smiled, tossed his matches to the young man.

'Thank you again,' Wyatt said and brought a flame to the smoke. He sucked the smoke in hard and allowed it to hiss free between his teeth. This seemed to ease some of the tension between the men. It could be felt leaving the room as if it were a tangible thing.

'There was no livestock here, the place looked deserted,' the kid continued, smoking as he spoke. 'I just thought I'd spend the winter here and then move on come spring and find some ranch that was hiring on men. Usually all the hiring's done by winter and I figured most ranches would have enough men until the drives started back up come spring.'

'Is that what you do? Cattle?'

'I'll pretty much try my hand at anything,' the kid said. 'But yeah it's mostly been cattle drives. I got a way with horses.'

It struck Johnny as odd that this kid could have been living here for close on a month without anyone in town being aware of it.

'You ain't been into town?' he asked.

'No.'

'What you been doing for food?' Johnny drew on the last of his smoke and tossed it into the unlit fireplace.

'I had some supplies with me when I got here,' the kid said. 'I still got me a full sack of Folgers and some dried beans. I do a little hunting, mostly jackrabbits. If I'm lucky I may bag myself a wild turkey or two.'

Johnny crossed the room and picked up the young man's gun belt.

'Tell you what,' he said. 'I reckon I'll keep this for the moment.'

The young man nodded. 'Sure. I don't guess I'll be needing it. I sure hope you ain't intending on using that rifle.'

'No,' Johnny said and placed his rifle down on the floor beside him. He still wore a gun belt, though he didn't feel the kid would be any trouble. He seemed an amiable enough fella, just a drifter, and that was sure enough something Johnny could identify with.

'I'm mighty pleased to hear that,' the kid said and drew on his smoke. 'You want me to pour you a coffee? There's still some in the pot on the stove.'

Johnny nodded, and when the kid handed him the tin mug he gulped the thick liquid down quickly. 'Obliged,' he said.

The kid filled a second tin mug of coffee and sat back on the edge of the cot, sipping at the hot beverage.

'So you own this place?' he asked.

Johnny nodded, said: 'It was my pa's. It's mine now.'

The kid drained his own coffee.

'It's a nice place,' he said.

'I aim to make it a prosperous place.' Johnny made himself another quirly and again offered his makings to the kid but he declined. 'I'm going to get me some stock. Horses mostly, and maybe try and breed some fine beasts I can then sell on.'

'Sounds a good idea,' the kid said.

Johnny suddenly felt drunk again and he picked up his rifle and then made his way to the bedroom. His hand paused on the door handle and he turned to look back at the young man.

'My horse is hitched outside,' he said. 'I'd be mighty obliged if you'd feed it and put it in the barn. We can talk in the morning.'

'Sure thing, mister.' The young man jumped to his feet, eager to be of service to the man whose home he had been using.

'Johnny. Call me Johnny.' With that Johnny went into the bedroom and within minutes was fast asleep, the alcohol he'd consumed and the long day just gone by combining into a powerful sedative.

4

Johnny awoke with the dawn, as had always been his habit. When he left the bedroom and went through to the main room of the ranch house he found Wyatt had already left. The kid's gun belt, though, remained just where Johnny had tossed it the previous night so he figured the kid wasn't too far away.

There was a small fire burning in the stove and a pot of delicious-smelling coffee on top. Johnny crossed the room, grabbed a tin cup from a hook on the wall and poured himself some. He took a sip, thinking the kid made damn fine coffee. He took it outside and stood in the open doorway and then he saw Wyatt come out of the barn and crossing towards the house. The kid was carrying a tool bag and he wore heavy leather gloves.

'Howdy,' Johnny said, and took another sip of the delicious coffee.

'It's gonna be a lovely day,' Wyatt said as he approached Johnny. 'Though it's getting colder. You can feel it in the air.'

Johnny nodded and looked up at the damn-near cloudless sky. There was paleness to the blue and although the sun was climbing it wasn't giving off that much in the way of heat. 'Winter ain't far off,' he concluded.

The kid nodded. It was true. You could feel it in the air.

'I've just been fixing up the barn,' he said.

'I'm obliged,' Johnny said. He took his makings from his shirt and after putting together a quirly he tossed them to the kid.

'Guess I'll be moving on,' the kid said, rolling a thin smoke for himself. 'I'd like to pay you for the use of your place. I ain't got much in the way of money but I figure the work I've done around here should even things up some. I've fixed up that old rickety fence behind the barn and before I go I reckon I'll finish patching up the barn roof. There's a few leaks here and there that could use some attention before the winter gets here, too.'

Johnny nodded, sipped his coffee.

'You make mighty fine coffee,' he said.

The kid smiled.

''Course, I'll be needing my rig before I go. Can't be riding around without a gun,' he said.

'You got a horse then?'

The kid nodded.

'She's in the barn. Like I say I didn't figure I was doing no harm, what with the place seeming deserted and all.'

'I ain't got no problem with you having stayed here,' Johnny said. 'It sure looks like you've done more good than harm.' He took another mouthful of the coffee.

'Well I'm mighty obliged to your attitude, mister.'

'Johnny,' Johnny corrected.

'Johnny.' The kid nodded, smiled again.

'Come inside,' Johnny said. 'Let's talk

this through. I could do with a hand around this place and if you take the job then you could stay on here. That's of course if you've got no place better to go.'

The young man grinned, smiled, said: 'I ain't got no place else to go for the moment. Better or worse.'

'I ain't got much in the way of money myself,' Johnny said. 'But I'm sure we can come to some arrangement.'

* * *

The two men had talked for an hour or so. They sat there at the old rickety table, the back legs of which Wyatt had repaired using timber found behind the barn, and smoked and drank coffee.

It was decided that Wyatt would indeed stay on for a period and that Johnny would pay him a fair wage as soon as he was solvent enough to do so. Until then the kid would get room and board and IOUs for the cash money. There was much to be done around the ranch and Johnny had big ideas for the place. He told the kid that he planned on putting his inheritance money, what little he was expecting, into the place. Maybe building up a herd of horses, keeping the best for breeding stock and selling the others on. There was a great demand for fine horses at the moment and it seemed the kid knew his way around a horse.

Johnny liked Wyatt and found the young man reminded him of himself. The kid was down on his luck and had nowhere to go, which was something Johnny sure knew a lot about. And, as he reminded himself almost daily, if Walt and Elisa Bren hadn't offered him the hand of kindness all those years ago then there was no telling which way his own life would have gone. These four walls around them now were only his because of that kindness given to a tiny abandoned baby and whilst Wyatt was far from a little bitty baby the principle was the same.

Afterwards Johnny said he had to

ride back into Jerusalem and meet with John Daggett, a lawyer who practised in town and would arrange for the remainder of Johnny's inheritance to be paid over to him. Johnny was hoping it would be enough to at least get himself a horse — he wanted to return Jessie Walker's horse as soon as possible. And Johnny reasoned that if he was lucky there might even be a bit of cash money left over to get some supplies for the ranch. The coffee they were drinking was Wyatt's, brought with him from his last job, and there was little in the way of food about the place.

'I'll maybe get a few chickens,' Johnny said after a long silence. 'They don't need much caring for and are hardy enough to survive the winter. That way I'll have eggs about the place. A few fresh eggs will make a good breakfast.'

Wyatt nodded and drew on his quirly.

'I'm going to turn this place around,' Johnny said. 'Raise some fine horses.' If there was one thing he knew about it was horses and he was sure he'd be able to make himself a comfortable living as a horse trader. There were still plenty of mavericks in the mountains not too far away that would give him a fine basis from which to build a good stock. Johnny planned on riding out and building himself up a herd before the month was out and Wyatt, who looked a strong and capable kid, would prove mighty handy to such a venture.

'Sounds like a solid plan,' the kid agreed.

'It's a plan, sure enough,' Johnny said, standing up and stretching a kink out of his back. 'But first I've got to go and see that damn lawyer.'

Wyatt said he'd accompany Johnny, figuring he'd like to see just what sort of town Jerusalem was. Makes sense to get acquainted with the town's folk, the kid had said, seeing as how it looked like he'd be staying around some.

5

Lawyer Daggett's office was at the extreme northern end of Main Street and after leaving Wyatt to take the horses into the livery stable, Johnny made his way directly there. The lawyer made him wait a few minutes in the outer office — Johnny guessed this was just for effect since the man didn't seem to be overly busy — before calling him in and inviting him to sit in one of the plush leather chairs.

'How are you?' Lawyer Daggett asked as he regarded Johnny over the rim of his glasses.

'Getting older,' Johnny said and took a pointed glance at the clock before catching the lawyer in a steely stare. He didn't remove his hat and instead sat there waiting for the lawyer to get about his business.

'Yes, well, we all are,' the lawyer said

and then cleared his throat. He reached into the pocket of his waistcoat and with a small brass key opened the top left drawer in his desk. He pulled out a document and, peering over his spectacles, regarded it for several moments before looking back at Johnny.

'It's all pretty straightforward,' he said.

'Pleased to hear that,' Johnny said. Straightforward was just how he liked things.

The lawyer gave the document another glance, though in truth there wasn't even any need for that since it was he himself who had drawn up the original document.

'I just need you to sign a few documents,' the lawyer said. 'I believe you've already taken possession of the ranch?'

Johnny nodded.

'Then there's a small matter of a financial sum to be paid and that closes the estate.'

'That's why I'm here,' Johnny said.

'Indeed.' The lawyer stood up and ran a hand over his portly stomach, which strained against the tightness of his clothing. He wasn't wearing his jacket, which was draped over the back of his chair. The stitching around the arms of his waistcoat was at such a strain that it looked as if it would burst at any moment. 'I'll just bring in my clerk to witness your signature and we can conclude our business.'

Johnny had always felt ill at ease in official situations. He smiled nervously, repeated: 'That's why I'm here.' The lawyer was long-winded and was starting to get on his nerves.

Lawyer Daggett left the room and returned a moment later with a smaller though equally rotund man in tow.

'This is Mr Charles Goodwich,' Lawyer Daggett said. 'He'll witness your signature, make everything legal and above board.'

Johnny nodded, said nothing.

Lawyer Daggett lowered himself back into his chair, picked up the document, cleared his throat and started to read out aloud.

'This being the last will and testament of Walter Enoch Bren . . . ' There followed a lot of legalese that became a drone to Johnny and he sat there, looking at the two officious men while most of the words being spoken didn't even register in his mind. There were a lot of 'bequeaths' and a few 'notwithstandings' and several 'herewiths', but then the sum of one thousand two hundred dollars was mentioned. This was to be adjusted, the lawyer pointed out, due to creditors having to be paid off, which included a significant sum owed to the town bank as well as administration and funeral costs. The figure was amended down to seven hundred and fifty dollars, which Johnny considered a small fortune and a lot more than he'd been expecting. Still, money meant little to him. He'd much rather have had Walt alive and well, but the sum sure wouldn't hurt and would go some way to getting the ranch back up and running.

'I need you to sign here, here and

here,' Lawyer Daggett concluded, pushing two documents across the table to Johnny. Next he handed him a dip pen and slid a small inkpot towards him.

Johnny signed and then handed the pen to the clerk, who signed the documents alongside Johnny's signature.

Lawyer Daggett smiled.

'There, that's our business almost concluded.' He reached back in his drawer and pulled out a letter, which was headed with the logo of the Jerusalem Bank and handed it to Johnny. 'Produce this at the town bank and they'll arrange for the money to be paid to you.'

'Thank you,' Johnny said and without looking at the letter he folded it and placed it in the breast pocket of his shirt. He stood up and shook both men's hands and then left the lawyer's office, grateful to be out of the cloying atmosphere and back into the early afternoon sunshine. Never had the breeze felt so good on his face than at that moment.

* * *

Main Street was pretty busy when Johnny stepped out and he saw Wyatt waving to him from the steps of the general store, which was situated right next to the Indian Creek Saloon. Johnny pushed his hat up slightly on his head and crossed the street. At that moment Jessie Walker came out of the saloon, noticed Johnny approaching and gave another of his big old fang-faced grins.

'Howdy,' Johnny said, tipping his hat to the old man and then pointing to the kid, who was watching the exchange with some amusement. 'This here's Wyatt. He's going to be working for me.'

'Pleased to meet you,' Jessie said, his smile widening even further. He pumped the kid's hand several times.

'I'm in a position to pay you for the loan of the horse.' Johnny spoke directly to the old man. 'Or will be just as soon as I visit the bank.'

'Don't offend me,' the old man said. 'I loaned you the horse out of kindness and friendship. I don't want no paying. Though I sure wouldn't say no to a drink or two.'

Johnny smiled.

'I'm obliged,' he said, and looked up and down the street. 'I'll be looking to buy a horse in any case.'

'And I'll give you a good price,' the old man said. 'That I can do. Come on, we'll discuss it over a drink.'

'Maybe later,' Johnny said, holding out the letter the lawyer had given him. He was aware that he had drunk a little too much yesterday and now that he had some money he sure didn't want to tempt fate. He'd done far too much drinking in the past and he wanted to face the future with a sober mind. 'I've got to call at the bank first.'

'Sure thing,' the old man said. 'I reckon the kid here can join me for a drink while we wait for you.'

'I'd not say no to that,' the kid said. 'Though I ain't got no money myself.'

'I'll stand you a drink,' the old man said and slapped the kid on the back. He turned to Johnny. 'You go about your business and you'll find us waiting with a drink for you when you're done. We'll talk about that horse then.'

'Once more I'm obliged to you.' Johnny took his makings from his pocket and quickly constructed a quirly.

The three men stood there for a moment while Johnny handed his makings around and each made themselves a smoke. The sheriff rode past but none of them even looked at him, nor did they notice the way the lawman regarded Wyatt. No doubt taking such deep interest because he was a new face in town. Didn't get that many new faces in Jerusalem.

'Well I'm going to conclude my business at the bank,' Johnny said and dropped his smoke into the dirt; he twisted it beneath a heel. Out of the corner of an eye he noticed Cherry Mewis crossing the street and he watched her as she went into the telegraph office. He wondered who she would be sending a telegraph to — a friend, a lover, perhaps? He scolded himself for the train of thought. Whatever Miss Mewis was up to it was none of his concern. Sooner he realized that the better.

'Well let's go get that drink,' the old man said and placed an arm over Wyatt's shoulder. He had noticed the way Johnny had been staring at the woman but had a little too much tact to say so. 'We'll be in the Indian Creek waiting for you.'

'Sure thing,' Johnny said, his mind half occupied with thoughts of the vision that was Cherry Mewis. He stood there for a moment after the old man and Wyatt had gone into the saloon and then shook his head, thinking that Cherry Mewis had sure grown into a beautiful young lady. There had been a time when Johnny had thought they would get hitched but that had been a long time ago, and a lot of muddy water had gone under the bridge between then and now.

'Damn.' He spat on to the ground and made his way to the town bank.

6

If anything the bank was even stuffier than the lawyer's office, and Johnny was pleased to discover that he was the only customer. The quicker he got his business done, the better. He regarded the letter in his hand for a moment before making his way to the bank clerk and pushing the paper across the counter.

The clerk, a middle-aged man with a bald, dome-like head and shifty-looking eyes quickly read the letter, and then looked at Johnny.

'Mr Carver will have to handle this,' he said. 'Wait here a moment please.'

Johnny nodded and watched the man scamper off to a back room. He returned a moment later accompanied by a tall, cadaverously thin man. Mr Carver, presumably. At the same moment the front doors opened and two elderly women entered. The clerk went to the next position on the counter to serve one of them, while the tall man came to Johnny. His limbs seemed ill coordinated and the way he moved reminded Johnny of a spider.

'You're Mr Jerusalem?' the tall man said.

Johnny nodded, aware that one of the old women was staring at him intently.

'Only name I've ever had,' he said and looked directly at the old woman who was regarding him so closely. She flushed and turned her gaze away from Johnny.

'I'm Thomas Carver, manager of this bank,' the man said and then asked: 'Do you want me to open an account in your name with this money?'

'No.' Johnny shook his head. 'Never had much to do with banks and don't intend to start now. I'll take the money.'

'This is a considerable sum, Mr Jerusalem.' Carver cleared his throat. 'Withdrawing such a sum may not be wise. Why, if I banked this money for you, or at least a part of it, then it would be earning you interest. Your money would be working for you.'

'The money,' Johnny said. This time his voice was firm with a hard edge that the banker didn't feel like arguing with.

'Very well.' Carver gave a slight smile. 'You know your mind, I see. You'll have to sign for it, of course.'

Johnny, who had never signed his name so many times in the same day, simply nodded. He noticed the old woman was once again looking up at him and he gave her a polite smile, figuring she must have recognized him from his name or his features. He wasn't sure if he'd ever seen the old woman before but he guessed she could have been someone he'd once known.

'I'll get the necessary paperwork,' Carver said.

Johnny nodded, said nothing. This was already taking too long.

Johnny's business took maybe ten minutes to conclude, during which time several more customers came in and by the time Johnny held the money in his hands, the bank was pretty busy and he was sure glad to be getting out of the building. It had been stuffy enough when he had been alone and now he didn't feel as if there was any air left at all. Johnny thanked the banker and turned to leave just as the front doors swung open and three masked gunmen entered. He stood perfectly still, not wanting to go for his guns and force a fight with so many other people about. He quickly slid the bundle of bank notes into his shirt.

The three gunmen were almost identical in size and dressed in a similar fashion. They wore black Levis and scarlet red shirts. Each of them had black bandannas pulled up over their mouths, and wore their hats down low over their foreheads so that all but their eyes were hidden from view. They were dressed, Johnny thought, like a dime novel version of a bank robber. These men would likely be called something like the Red Shirt Bunch or some other such nonsense.

'Do as I say,' one of the gunmen, obviously the leader, said. 'And ain't nobody gonna get hurt.' He turned to Johnny and aimed his gun directly at his head while his two partners covered the rest of the room. 'Unhitch that gun belt, let it drop to the floor and kick it towards me.'

'You won't get no trouble from me,' Johnny drawled.

'Unhitch the gun belt,' the man shouted, an audible quiver in his voice. 'I'd feel a whole lot easier with that gun gone.'

Johnny kept eye contact with the man as his hands went to his belt buckle. He carefully unhitched the clasp and allowed his gun to fall to the floor, noticing as he did so that the bandit holding the gun on him was shaking, obviously nervous, which made him all the more dangerous. The man's nerves were clearly at breaking point and were likely to snap with the slightest provocation. Whoever these men were they sure didn't seem like seasoned robbers.

'Good.' There was relief in the gunman's voice. 'Now kick the rig towards me. Slowly. No sudden movements.'

Johnny did so. The gunman crossed the room and, keeping his gun trained on Johnny, he used the back of his heel to kick the gun belt towards his own men. Johnny heard one of the other men ordering everyone but the bank manager to come around from behind the counter and lay on the floor, face down, with their hands behind their heads, and the man who had his gun trained on Johnny turned to see what was happening behind him. A stupid mistake and for a moment Johnny considered lunging at the gunman, hoping to take him by surprise and wrestle the gun from him but he decided against it. The gunman was shaking worse than ever, his finger seeming to tremble on the trigger, and Johnny kept his eye trained on the gun, hoping the man's shaking wouldn't send a slug his way.

'Come on, move,' one of the bandits shouted and the clerk and a woman emerged from the door to the left of the counter and stood next to the bank's customers. The gunmen looked at each other, as though not knowing what to do. They had everyone in the bank under control and yet it seemed as if they had no clear idea what came next.

'Get down on the floor,' one of the gunmen shouted, panic in his voice.

'Not you,' the gunman holding the gun on Johnny said. 'One move and I'll shoot you where you stand.'

Johnny gave the gunman a thin smile.

'I told you,' he said. 'You won't get no trouble from me.'

The gunman nodded and moved a little closer to Johnny. He reached out with his free hand and frisked Johnny.

'What's this?' he asked as he felt the bulk beneath Johnny's shirt. He reached into the shirt and pulled out the bundle of notes that totalled seven hundred and fifty dollars.

'That's mine,' Johnny said and made to move forward but the bandit stepped back and Johnny saw his finger tense on the trigger. That stopped Johnny dead in his tracks. 'That's my money.'

'It's our money now,' the gunman said and pushed the wad of notes into his own shirt.

'You.' One of the gunmen moved to the counter and pointed his gun directly at Carver. 'Put all the money from your safe in this sack.' He pulled a sack from beneath his shirt and tossed it on the counter. 'Do it quickly and this'll all be over without anyone getting hurt.'

One of the customers, actually the old woman, who had displayed such an interest in Johnny, started to scream and the gunman closest to her directed a brutal kick to the side of her face.

The shock of the blow silenced her immediately. Johnny suddenly lunged forward and managed to take the man who had been holding the gun on him by surprise. Johnny pushed the man backwards and at the same time delivered a punishing left hook to the man's jaw. The man went down immediately, his legs buckling beneath him and Johnny dived for the man's gun but one of the other men came forward and brought his own gun down hard on the back of Johnny's head.

Johnny felt intense pain and then blackness overcame him.

★   ★   ★

'Let's get this done,' the bandit yelled, turning from Johnny. 'Everyone else get up off the floor and move against the wall and you,' he directed his last to Carver, 'fill that sack and we'll be gone from here. One wrong move and we'll blow you all away.'

Another of the bank's customers started to scream but a bandit quickly crossed the room and backslapped her forcefully across the face.

'Shut up,' the bandit leader snapped. 'Let's get this done.'

Two of the bandits made their way to the bank counter while the other stayed by the door, his guns covering the bank.

'Open the strong box and fill that sack,' the gunman at the counter again ordered and this time the bank manager moved to comply with the command.

7

It was the sound of gunfire that brought Johnny around. He tried to push himself to his feet and immediately had to double up as he vomited on to the floor. He wiped the spittle from his lips and got to his knees, looking around in confusion. His head was swimming after the blow and he felt sick again but this time he managed to bite it back.

'They're out there, mister,' the tall thin banker said. 'By the sound of it they've met a welcoming party.'

Johnny managed to get to his feet. He stood there and looked around for a moment. Other than the bandits no one else seemed to have left the bank. Both of the bankers were gathered with the customers as they fought for the window and a view of what was going on outside. Suddenly the glass was smashed and a bullet powered into the wall behind Johnny, fine wood splinters filling the air. After that, no one went anywhere near the window.

Johnny, remembering the money the bandit had taken from him, turned to leave and noticed his gun belt was still on the floor. On unsteady feet he went to the rig and placed it on.

He grabbed his Colt, checked it was still loaded and made his way to the door.

'Wait, mister,' someone yelled. 'It's a fire fight out there.'

Johnny ignored the warning and went to the door. He swung it open and stepped outside but had to hit the ground when a bullet exploded into the doorframe, spitting up another cloud of splinters. He noticed that it had been Sheriff Banson, no doubt mistaking him for a fourth bandit, who had fired.

'Wait!' Johnny yelled.

He saw the three bandits, now on horseback, nearing the end of Main Street and he let off a wild shot in their direction. It was pure luck but the shot struck home, entering the bandit between the shoulder blades and sending out a spray of crimson. The bandit arched his back, screamed and then fell from his horse, dead before he hit the ground. The other bandits didn't even look back and their horses left behind a cloud of dust as they vanished into the distance.

'Damn fine shot,' a voice said as Johnny felt hands reaching and helping him to his feet. He saw it was Wyatt, the kid's face blood-splattered.

'You been hit?' Johnny asked.

'No,' Wyatt said and pointed across the street to where a prone figure lay on the ground. Johnny knew immediately that it was the old man.

'The old man's dead,' Wyatt said. 'He was the first one to get it.'

The bandits had killed Jessie Walker. Now it wasn't only the question of the money; the old man had been good to him and Johnny knew there and then that he wouldn't rest until he had caught up with those bandits, served his own particular brand of justice on them.

'You OK?' Sheriff Banson had come across and was looking at Johnny with concern. He still held his smoking gun in his hand.

'Yeah,' Johnny said and again looked at the prone figure of Jessie Walker.

The sheriff nodded, reading Johnny's eyes.

'Yeah, the old man's dead.' He looked across at Wyatt and then pointed his gun at him. 'You stay there,' he said.

'He's with me,' Johnny said, stepping between Wyatt and the sheriff. 'He ain't no part of this.'

'Where's he hail from?' the sheriff asked, regarding Wyatt with suspicion. 'He weren't with you when you came into town yesterday. First time I saw him was this morning and a couple of hours later this happens.'

Johnny looked at Wyatt and then at the sheriff.

'He's with me,' he repeated.

'Mighty strange a new face being in town on the day of a robbery.' Banson caught Wyatt's eyes and held them in

65

his stare. 'That seems quite a coincidence.'

'He's with me,' Johnny repeated once again. He watched as the sheriff holstered his weapon. Johnny did likewise and then he and the kid ran to the old man.

Johnny knelt beside the body and gently, as though not wanting to hurt the old man, even though he was well past feeling any pain, he turned him over. There was no question now that he was dead — there was a bloody wound in the centre of his throat where a slug had entered. He would have died instantly.

'Those men came out of the bank and then all hell broke loose,' Wyatt said. 'The old man tried to put up a fight with that scattergun he carried, but one of the bandits got him with a rifle.'

Johnny closed the old man's eyes and feeling tears forming in his own, he wiped them with the back of his sleeve.

'You got one of the *hombres*, though,' Wyatt said.

Johnny nodded, crossed the now packed street to where the bandit had fallen.

'He got anything on him?' Johnny asked the sheriff who was kneeling by the corpse and had already searched him.

'No.' The sheriff stood up and wiped his brow with the back of a gloved hand. 'I'll get a posse together and go after the other two.'

'You can count me in,' Johnny said.

'And me.' Wyatt gave the sheriff a tight smile.

'I ain't yet sure you're nothing to do with this.' The sheriff spoke directly to Wyatt. 'We don't get many new faces in Jerusalem and I find you being here mighty strange to my lawman sensibilities.'

'Those lawman sensibilities are barking up the wrong tree,' Johnny said and spat on to the dead bandit. 'I've already told you the kid's with me.'

The sheriff nodded, spat himself and then looked around the crowded street. 'Any of you townsmen want to join a posse,' he said, 'get heeled up and mounted and be outside my office in thirty minutes.' With that he pushed through the gathered crowd and crossed the street towards his own office.

Johnny noticed the crowd of people looked to be more concerned with gawping at the bandit's body than with the old man who had lived among them and was now lying dead in the dirt.

The town undertaker turned up. He led his horse and cart to the edge of the crowd and then went to the dead bandit. He laid a thin blanket on the ground with which he would wrap the body, but Johnny grabbed him by the scruff of the neck and lifted him up.

'Leave him,' Johnny said. 'Let the flies get him. Take care of the old man first.'

For a moment the undertaker seemed about to protest but something in Johnny's eyes convinced him otherwise. He nodded and led his horse and cart back towards the body of Jessie Walker.

'You make sure you give him the best

casket you got,' Johnny said, walking behind the undertaker. 'And a marker. He'll be wanting a fine market on his grave.'

The undertaker turned and set his sad eyes on Johnny.

'The old man ain't got no kin,' he said. 'That kind of service don't come cheap.'

'Bill me,' Johnny said. 'Whatever it costs. I'll make sure you get your money.'

For a moment the undertaker looked as if he was going to argue but again he thought better of it. He nodded his head and looked down at the old man.

'I'm sorry for your loss,' he said and set about his professional duties.

'Sure,' Johnny said.

He reached up and felt the goose egg that had formed on the back of his head. He still had a pounding in the back of his skull but it was getting more manageable. Just as well really, since he intended on riding out after the remaining bandits just as soon as he could.

★ ★ ★

There was pandemonium now that the danger was over. Curious onlookers came and stood in the street, many of them bunching together, forming clusters around Main Street. They talked amongst themselves, some of them relating what they had seen, many of them telling of things they knew nothing about, exaggerating events they had heard third hand. They watched as the undertaker removed first one body and then returned for the other.

Johnny stood there in the middle of the street for a few moments, the kid next to him. Finally he shook his head, spat into the dirt and started across the street.

8

Feeling the need for a stiff drink, and this time not arguing with himself over the need, Johnny went into the Indian Creek while Wyatt went to the livery stable to get their horses saddled up and ready to ride.

'Some excitement out there today,' the barkeep said as he slid the whiskey across the counter. 'Can't remember the last time we had a gunfight in Jerusalem.'

Johnny took a sip of the strong liquor, nodded but said nothing. It had been a long time since he'd drunk whiskey and he could feel it burning in his stomach.

'Heard the bank was held up,' the barkeep continued, wiping the inside of a glass with a filthy rag while he spoke. 'Wouldn't have thought a two-bit, one-horse town like this would attract much in the way of desperadoes.'

'You never can tell,' Johnny said. He was in no mood for conversation and he quickly drained his drink. He considered having another but then turned on his heels and went back outside.

Wyatt, leading the horses, came across the street having to negotiate his way past the crowds.

'Guess we'd better go see the sheriff,' Johnny said and took the reins of his own horse from the kid. Only it wasn't his own horse, he remembered. It had belonged to Jessie Walker but given the tragic circumstances he guessed he owned it now. It looked as if it wasn't only seven hundred and fifty dollars Johnny had inherited today.

'Don't think he trusts me,' Wyatt muttered.

'Don't think Hoss much trusts anyone,' Johnny said. 'I wouldn't take it personal. Sometimes I reckon that fella don't even trust himself.'

'Be careful, Mr Jerusalem.' The voice came from behind them and startled the two men. Johnny turned around and saw the familiar face of Cherry Lee Mewis. She had been standing talking with two other women, and now she walked forward and looked at both Johnny and Wyatt.

'You used to call me Johnny,' he said.

The woman blushed slightly and then smiled.

'That was a long time ago,' she said and looked up and down the street. 'Mr Jerusalem seems more fitting.'

'Sure,' Johnny agreed. 'But don't you worry none about us. I can take care of myself and I'm sure young Wyatt here's got enough sand to do likewise.'

'You're riding with the posse?' the woman asked and Johnny was sure he detected a hint of genuine concern in her eyes. Maybe whatever it was they had had between them was not as far in the past as he'd imagined.

'They took my money as well as the bank's,' Johnny said. 'But that ain't it. They killed old man Walker and they've got to answer for that. He was friendly with my pa and he did me a kindness when I got back into town. I'm beholden to the old man and I guess the only way I can pay that debt is to run down his killers and make sure they get what's coming to them.'

A look of sadness crossed the woman's face and she nodded her understanding. That was something she understood: blood had to be answered with blood in this godforsaken country.

'Just be careful,' she said. 'Come back alive. Those bandits have had enough luck as it is.'

'Luck?' Johnny felt that was a curious thing to say and he looked deep into the woman's eyes. 'They lost one of their own. I wouldn't call that luck.'

'Of course not,' Cherry said. 'But hitting the bank just when there was so much extra money held there. They couldn't have known that, of course, but for them their timing must have proved fortuitous.'

Johnny and Wyatt exchanged a puzzled glance. The woman had lost them now and they had no idea what she was talking about. Extra money? Why should the bank be holding more money than was usual?

'I don't follow you,' Johnny said.

'Government money, a lot of it. The Indian compensation payouts,' Cherry said and then took a furtive look around. 'The Indians over at the Indian Creek Reservation were getting government compensation for the lands taken when the railroad came. It's been a long time coming; some folk don't think the Indians are entitled to any recompense for their land and for a long time it seemed the government were taking the same stance. But after what happened to General Custer I don't think the military have the stomach for another Indian uprising. The army delivered the funds to the bank earlier in the week.'

'And the bandits couldn't have known this?'

'No.' Cherry shook her head. 'I only know because I work in the bank from time to time. 'Course, folk were curious as to why the army had been in town but as far as I know the news didn't get out.'

'How much?' Johnny asked. 'How much was held in the bank?'

'I'm not sure of that,' Cherry said. 'I wasn't privy to that knowledge but the compensation package was believed to be considerable. None of it had been paid out yet so whoever those robbers were they likely got away with a vast amount of money.'

'And you're certain the bandits couldn't have known about the money?' Johnny asked.

Cherry shook her head. 'No,' she said. 'It wasn't public knowledge and other than the bank staff the only person who knew about the money was the sheriff.'

'Sons of bitches struck lucky,' Wyatt said and then smiled apologetically when he saw the frown Johnny had thrown his way. He quickly added: 'Excuse my cussing, miss.'

★ ★ ★

'I've changed my mind,' Johnny said. 'We'll ride out ahead of the posse.'

'We ain't waiting for the sheriff, then?' Wyatt asked, pulling himself into the saddle.

'Hell no,' Johnny said. 'There's a lot of country out there and by the time Hoss gets things organized those bandits will be long gone.'

'I don't know the man,' Wyatt said. 'But from what I've seen I don't think he'll be happy us going off like our own little posse.'

'Hoss ain't ever happy,' Johnny replied. 'Don't see that ever changing.' After what Cherry Mewis had said Johnny wasn't at all sure he could trust the sheriff. Maybe he was somehow involved in the robbery, and from what Johnny knew of Banson he sure wouldn't put that beyond him. The sheriff had known about the considerable money in the bank and those bandits had seemed like amateurs; they'd all been shaking in their boots, like they didn't know one end of a gun from the other. Maybe someone in the know had put them up to the robbery; maybe they weren't seasoned bandits at all.

Immediately following the conversation with Cherry Mewis, they had gone to the general store where Johnny had opened up a line of credit. The storekeeper, a kindly faced man named Jim White, commonly called Whitey, knew Johnny of old and was only too happy to extend him credit. They'd purchased provisions for their pursuit of the two bandits — 'Best be prepared,' Johnny had said. 'No telling how long we'll be chasing those varmints' — and when they left town their saddle-bags were loaded up with coffee, jerky, beans, biscuits, tobacco and extra ammunition.

Although Wyatt felt uneasy and would have much preferred to ride along with the official posse, he spurred his horse off after Johnny, and within minutes the two men had left town and were heading out into the wilderness.

'How long till you figure we'll catch

up with those bandits?' the kid asked, breaking a silence that had fallen between them.

Johnny shrugged his shoulders, keeping his eyes directed down at the ground. He could see from the tracks the bandits had left behind that they were moving at considerable speed, but a horse couldn't keep to that pace for too many miles. It was likely that somewhere up ahead the bandits had slowed to a more considered speed, least they would have to if they didn't want to run their horses into the ground.

'Guess we'll catch them when we catch them,' he finally said.

The kid looked at Johnny and for a moment it looked as if he was going to continue the conversation, but instead he simply shrugged and spurred his horse to keep it level with Johnny's.

9

'Son of a bitch.' The sheriff ground his teeth together, something he always did when irritated. Being informed, by the saloon-keeper, that Johnny Jerusalem and the kid he'd partnered up with had already ridden out of town had sure stoked up his ire.

'He's only just arrived back in town and already he's off taking the law into his own hands. I'll whip his fool hide when we catch up with him,' the sheriff said, speaking more to himself than any of the other men with him.

The five men in the sheriff's posse said nothing, merely sat on their horses and waited for the sheriff to give the order to ride out. It wasn't much of a posse, made up of townsmen, the majority of whom didn't know one end of a rifle from the other. Holding his horse steady alongside the sheriff's was

Clive Longmire, the town's blacksmith. A man whose burly hands, fingers like thick sausages, were much better suited to bending steel than holding iron. The remaining four men in the posse were Jim and Sam, otherwise known as the Clemens brothers, Henry Wayne, who usually made his living from hiring himself out as a handyman and Walt Cartwright, who had ridden with General Sherman during the war. Back then he'd been a force to be reckoned with, but these days his arthritic fingers were next to useless when it came to a fight. Nope, it sure wasn't much of a posse but it was all the town of Jerusalem could muster.

'Let's go,' the sheriff yelled, turning his horse so quickly that it kicked up a riot of dust and stone. 'We're burning daylight. Let's ride these *hombres* down.'

Someone in the posse let out a 'Yeehaw'. The sheriff figured it had likely been one of the Clemens boys, since they were the only ones young and foolhardy enough.

The sun was low, almost kissing the horizon and looking like a wound in the sky, casting a blood-red glow that gave the landscape an almost ethereal sheen. The distant hills were blackly ragged in contrast.

The sheriff set the pace, which was not far short of a gallop. He wanted to cover as much ground as possible as quickly as possible and there was perhaps an hour left to them before darkness. And although the lawman intended to ride well into the night he knew that they'd have to slow right down as soon as the visibility lessened, either that or risk running the horses lame.

* * *

'We camp here,' Johnny said and slid from his horse. His legs were aching, his back was aching, and even his head was aching. He ground tied the horse and then sat down on a large rock before taking his makings from his shirt pocket.

'I figured we'd ride through the night,' the kid said.

'We camp here,' Johnny mumbled as he brought a match to the quirly he'd put together. 'We'll set off at first light.'

'But we could catch up with those varmints if we keep going,' the kid protested, speaking from his saddle.

'A lot of rough ground to cover,' Johnny said, allowing a stream of blue-grey smoke to escape from the corners of his mouth. 'We'll catch those fellas soon enough.'

'You sure of that?'

Johnny nodded, said simply: 'We camp here.'

'Guess we're camping here, then,' the kid said, patting his horse as he dismounted. He took the makings offered by Johnny and sat down on the edge of the rock. He quickly put together a quirly and lit it with a thick match, again supplied by Johnny.

They set a fire but kept it small so as not to attract the attention of the men they followed. They both figured that the men would be a good ways off, too far away to pick out the smoke in the night sky, but all the same Johnny felt that they should show caution. Soon the delicious aroma of coffee filled the air and Johnny put a couple of handfuls of dried beans into a pan and poured a little water over them. The supper of coffee, beans and jerky may have been basic but both men wolfed it down as if it were the last meal they'd ever have. There was little conversation between them while they ate and afterwards they each sat back, smoking and staring at the star-studded sky.

'Do you think the sheriff and his posse will be far behind us?' the kid asked, presently.

Johnny shrugged his shoulders. He had no idea and was still having trouble accepting the fact that Hoss Banson was now town sheriff. If there was any man who seemed a less likely lawman then Johnny had yet to meet him.

Hoss Banson was just shy of a year older than Johnny and although the two had never been real friends they had grown up together and in a town as small as Jerusalem it was nigh on impossible to totally avoid each other. Johnny had never really taken to Banson and remembered him as being a slovenly child. At school he had tried to intimidate the smaller pupils but would never stand his ground if someone turned on him; Hoss Banson had always been something of coward. Johnny still recalled the time when Hoss had tried to push him around. They'd been about ten years old then and Johnny had whipped Banson behind the schoolhouse, blackening both eyes and splitting his lower lip. The schoolmaster had come and broken it up, holding each boy at arm's length, while they both cartwheeled their own arms as if they were possessed. Johnny had been punished for this, six swipes with a rattan cane, but the chastisement had been worth it and with each swipe of that cane Johnny had been comforted by the mental image of Hoss Banson's bruised and battered face.

'I ain't got much faith in the sheriff,' Johnny said and flicked his quirly into the fire. It was received hungrily by the flames and almost immediately ceased to exist.

'Is that why we're out here alone?'

Johnny looked at the kid and once again he considered the possibility that the sheriff had somehow been involved in the robbery. The thought was constantly nagging away at the back of his mind, but he didn't want to talk about it until he was sure. The men holding up the bank had been trembling as they'd gone about the robbery, hadn't seemed at all comfortable with what they were doing, as though it was the first job they'd ever attempted. That bothered Johnny a little, and added to the fact that Cherry Mewis had mentioned the unusually large sum of money held in the bank, and how so few people knew it was there, it bothered him quite a lot. If the sheriff was involved in the robbery, then Johnny reasoned that his posse was just for effect. The lawman would make a show of going after the bandits but would make damn sure they got clean away. Banson could then meet up with the men at a later date and collect his cut of the proceeds. Least, that was Johnny's theory and the fact that he had no real basis for the hypothesis, only suspicions, didn't seem to matter. He didn't like the sheriff, didn't trust the sheriff and that was the reason he had ridden out ahead of the posse. Those bandits had killed old man Walker, as well as stolen all the money Johnny had in the world, and he was going to ensure they got what was coming to them. And if it did turn out that the sheriff was involved in the robbery then the lawman would get the same treatment. Johnny would make sure the lawman got his comeuppance and it wouldn't be no cut of the stolen money. Sure he'd get paid off but it would be in lead, hot lead.

'I don't figure I need the sheriff around,' he said. 'Guess that's enough reason for us riding out ahead of the posse.'

'He sure seemed the quarrelsome sort,' the kid observed.

'I guess you could say that.' Johnny pulled the collar of his jacket up and pushed his hat forward. He got himself as comfortable as he could, sitting on the ground and leaning back against the large rock. 'Yep, I guess you could say that.'

Somewhere in the distance an owl hooted and the kid poured the last of the coffee from the pot into his tin cup. He sipped it slowly, listening to the night sounds and thinking of the two men they would soon catch up with.

Sure enough, there was a reckoning coming.

10

Dawn was peppering the far horizon when Johnny gave the kid a foot-shaped alarm call. With the tip of his boot he gently kicked the kid in the back. Wyatt opened his eyes and ran a hand through his hair. He felt the morning's keen chill and was grateful for the coffee Johnny handed him. He shivered as he brought the tin cup to his mouth.

'We'll move out once you drink that coffee,' Johnny said. 'I'll ready the horses.'

The kid nodded, sipped the coffee. It was warm and sweet and he'd never tasted better. He moved closer to the small camp-fire that Johnny had coaxed back to life while he had been sleeping and enjoyed its warmth upon his face. It felt good against his skin and he turned so that his back could get some of the heat.

'Reckon we'll catch up with those varmints today?' the kid asked.

'Reckon so,' Johnny said without looking up from the task he was performing. He checked the straps on the saddle by pulling them tightly and gently patted his horse.

'And the sheriff?'

'Guess he won't be far behind,' Johnny said and pushed himself up into the saddle. 'Get that coffee down you. Let's git going.'

The kid downed the remainder of the coffee in one and shook the cup out over the fire. He went to his own horse and wearily climbed into the saddle.

Johnny tossed his makings across to the kid and placed the thin quirly he'd made between his own lips.

'A smoke'll help wake you up,' Johnny said, grinning at the kid.

'Obliged,' the kid said and quickly put together a smoke. 'I feel as if I've been torn from my bed and thrown on to my horse.' He tossed the makings back to Johnny and spurred his horse gently forwards.

They'd ridden on for several hours before Johnny found definite signs that the two riders they pursued had been this way. He had developed reasonable tracking skills over the years and could read things from the ground that others missed. His life on the move had made such skills, the ability to see a leaf out of place, or notice the small difference in the colour of a waterhole, of paramount importance. In his years away from Jerusalem Johnny had not amassed the fortune he'd hoped for but he had honed his skills and was just as comfortable out of doors as he was with a roof over his head. Sometimes more so.

Johnny held his horse steady while he considered the route the two men were taking; they were heading up into the mountain range, which made no sense since that way presented an arduous and dangerous trail. The mountains may have stretched clean across several territories, covering more than a thousand miles in total, with varying climates, but if the bandits wanted to put as much space as was possible between them and the town of Jerusalem then there were better routes, easier routes, quicker routes they could have taken. Surely they should have been heading out of the mountains and down to the Bute River, which would lead them on to the Great Plains, where several options for escape would be available to them. None of this made any sense and Johnny scratched his head and spat on to the ground. What kind of fools were these men they were pursuing? Johnny supposed they could have a bolt hole, a hideout, but again it made little sense that the men should not flee to the East and the relative safety that option offered. It was possible, Johnny supposed, that the bandits thought the law would be reluctant to follow them into the mountains.

The mountains that hid rogue Indians and cut-throat bandits.

Johnny didn't like this.

He didn't like this at all.

Of course, there was yet another possibility and maybe there was a perfectly sound reason for the men to be heading up into the mountains. Maybe they were going to hide out, wait for someone, that someone who had aided them in the robbery. That was another theory troubling Johnny and one that added more credence to the suggestion that the sheriff was involved in all this.

'We need to take extra caution from here on,' he said, pulling his horse to a stop and turning in his saddle to look at the kid. If the two men did have a hideout in the mountains then there was a chance that they would be planning an ambush, that they were aware they were being pursued and considered fighting to be a better option than running.

The kid nodded but said nothing.

Johnny and the kid continued up into the mountains, feeling the air thinning as their altitude increased. They went through a wooded area, taking caution else the bandits be concealing themselves in the dense woodland and waiting for them, but after an hour or perhaps more they found themselves riding along grassy banks that continued ever upwards. High above them Johnny could see several specks circling in the sky and although positive identification was impossible he thought they were turkey buzzards. Not a good sign and he took the birds to be a bad omen. It wasn't that Johnny was particularly superstitious but past experience had taught him that quite often the birds would show up before a killing. It was as if the birds had some sixth sense, an ability to detect great violence before it occurred.

Johnny took his horse over a patch of uneven ground and the climb started to steepen. He cast a look over his shoulder and found the kid was keeping up fine. They continued on like this for some time, both men cursing their horses as the beasts stumbled over the ever-tricky ground but then patting them soothingly as yet another obstacle was covered. Gradually the day grew warmer and this presented its own problems as the relentless climb took its toll on the horses.

'Best we lead the horses for a ways,' Johnny said, climbing from the saddle. 'Don't want to tire them out needlessly.'

'Pretty hard going,' the kid grumbled as he climbed from his own horse. There wasn't a muscle in his body that didn't seem to ache. 'You sure we're on the right trail?'

Johnny knelt and examined the ground. The men were doing little to hide their trail and a blind man could follow them easily enough. That was something else that worried him.

'We're following them,' Johnny said. 'They sure ain't making it hard for us neither. They're leaving more tracks than a herd of buffalo.'

'You figure they may be waiting for us?'

'That's what I figure,' Johnny said. 'That's exactly what I figure.'

The kid cleared leather, spun the chamber of his pistol and placed it back into its holster. He then patted the stock of the Winchester in his saddle boot.

'I'm ready for any trouble,' he said.

Johnny checked his own weapons and then took the makings from his shirt pocket. He made himself another smoke and tossed the makings to the kid.

'Just keep you ears and eyes open,' Johnny said and led his horse further into the mountains.

* * *

Sheriff Hoss Banson heard the scream and in one fluid motion he cleared leather and spun his horse around. At first he was confused, seeing nothing untoward with his posse, but then he noticed Sam Clemens sitting red-faced in his saddle.

'What the hell?' Banson cursed.

'Sorry Hoss,' Sam said. 'Critter took me by surprise.'

'Critter?'

'Yeah.' Sam pointed to the gelatinous

96

mess on his left sleeve. He had a disgusted look on his face as he rubbed it from his arm with a gloved hand. 'Damn spider took me by surprise is all.'

Several of them men started to laugh but their hilarity was cut short by a look of anger from the sheriff.

'We're on a damn man hunt,' he said. 'Not some Sunday afternoon ride.'

'Damn thing took me by surprise is all,' Sam said again, and gave an apologetic shrug of his shoulders.

'Shut up and ride,' the sheriff snapped. He shook his head and spurred his horse forward.

It sure as hell wasn't much of a posse and the sheriff was starting to think that the men with him were more of a burden than anything else, that he would be better off alone. He wanted to catch up with Johnny Jerusalem before they ran down the bandits. It just wouldn't do if Jerusalem, a man who had only just ridden back into town, managed to stop the bandits and retrieve the bank's money. There were folk in town who were criticizing Banson's style of keeping the peace, and even some who said he wasn't fit to wear the tin star. If anyone returned the town's money then he should be the one to do so. He was the elected town sheriff and Johnny Jerusalem was little more than a saddle-bum, a hopeless drifter.

The sheriff pulled a plug of chewing tobacco from his shirt pocket and bit off a good-sized lump. He chased it around his mouth for several moments before spitting out a stream of sepia-coloured saliva. He shifted in the saddle and spurred his horse forward, hoping that the fools behind him would be able to keep his pace. They didn't have time to waste, not if he wanted to catch up with Jerusalem, which in the sheriff's mind had become just as important, maybe more so, than catching up with the bandits.

Walt Cartwright pushed his own horse forward and pulled up level with the sheriff. He gave the lawman a tight smile and pushed his hat back slightly on his head.

'I know this ground,' he said. 'I've hunted out here and things are going to get a whole lot harder before too long.'

The sheriff, himself no stranger around these parts, nodded.

'These fellas are taking a strange route if you ask me,' the veteran soldier said. He had come to much the same conclusion as Johnny before him and he was of the mind that the bandits would set an ambush somewhere up ahead. 'You considered we might be riding into an ambush?'

'I have,' the sheriff said.

'Well I sure am glad you're aware of the possibility,' the old man said.

The sheriff looked at Cartwright for a moment and then gave a tight grin. He turned in the saddle and yelled: 'Come on, you men.'

Banson coaxed more speed out of his horse, once again taking the lead. They were heading towards the mountain range, and the lawman was only too aware that they wouldn't be able to maintain this speed in the mountains, but he didn't want to slow down none until they had to.

11

The two men didn't know what hit them. They were aware of the men in pursuit and had planned on setting up an ambush just as soon as they'd reached a location suitable, but they had been unprepared for the trouble that came from ahead of them.

It took them by surprise.

Not that they would have had a chance, had they been ready, for they were two guns, no match for the ten-strong party of Indians that attacked as soon as the men reached the area the whites called Pinshon Pass, so named for Edward Pinshon, a man who had mapped the mountains some years ago, but which the Indians knew as *Kte Oyate*, which translated roughly as Dead Nation. To the Lakota Indians this was sacred ground; legend told that the first of the Lakota people had lived here long ago, before the land had fully formed, in a time when the birds of the skies, and the beasts of the forest spoke, just as men today spoke. It was a time when man was just another part of nature and did not seek to dominate, to shape it to his own design. The ground here was made up of rock, mostly argillite that would give off a red glow when the sun hit it in a certain way and the Indians, being superstitious by nature, attributed this to the presence of the spirits of their people who had taken the journey from the physical life to a higher state of being.

'Indians,' the leader of the two men yelled and pulled the rifle from its boot, but before he could take aim an arrow thudded into his throat. He threw his arms up, dropping the rifle. Blood bubbled from his mouth, which was open in a silent scream as he fell backwards off his horse.

The second man tried to turn his horse and make an escape, letting off a shot as he did so, but he too was thrown from his horse when an arrow found him between the shoulder blades. He was still alive when he hit the ground and he gritted his teeth against the pain, which was mercifully cut short as another arrow split the back of his skull and pierced his brain, killing him instantly.

The Indians, a war party, ten braves in strength, whooped and hollered as they sent their horses into the small valley where the two white men lay dead. The leader of the war party, a Hunkpapa Lakota known as Charging Bear, took the vanguard and when he pulled his horse to a stop the braves behind him did so also. They held their steeds steady while they waited for the order to see whatever spoils they had gained from the two white men.

Charging Bear sat on his horse, a magnificent-looking white stallion, sniffing the wind as he looked at the two dead white men. He had the high cheekbones and impressive Roman nose common to his people, but his eyes were of the darkest brown and had been inherited from his mother, who had been born into the Comanche people of New Mexico. Years before he had been born the tribe had joined the Lakota people after their homelands had been taken over by the Spanish.

Charging Bear smiled at the sight of the two dead men.

He hated the whites, although there had been a time when he had given up his feud with them, decided that it was better for his own people if they made peace rather than continue to wage war. Then he had adopted the name John Grass and had sat at the negotiation table and worked to heal the wounds of war. For a time he had been successful and had worked hard for his people, discovering he was a skilled and natural politician. He had met with many white leaders and gained respect from these men, winning concessions for his people and ensuring they were treated fairly. And for a time it had seemed as if the troubles of the past were well and truly over, that the bloodshed had finally ceased. However, the old wounds were torn cruelly open when his young daughter of only fifteen summers was raped and then murdered by a drunken soldier at the reservation. From that day forward he had reverted to his warrior name, he had shed the trappings that went with John Grass, a man who existed in two cultures, he had once again become Charging Bear, a man who fought and killed for the survival of only one culture.

Charging Bear raised a hand and held it steady for a moment, before throwing it forward. He let out a blood-curdling scream of victory and once again his men started whooping and hollering as they leapt from their horses and went to search the dead men.

* * *

Johnny and Wyatt had heard the gunshot and figured it had come from less than a mile ahead of them. For a long while after the sound had faded they waited, expecting more gunfire to follow but all they heard was silence, save for the gentle hum of the wind.

'What do you think?' the kid asked Johnny, who was currently sat in the saddle, puffing thoughtfully on a quirly.

Johnny looked at the kid but said nothing for a moment. The fact that there had only been a single shot could mean many things. Maybe the bandits had come across a critter of some sort and had blasted it, either for the pot or because it had presented a danger to them. It could also mean that one of the men had turned on the other, but Johnny didn't think that likely, not with a posse in pursuit. Whatever the reason for the gunshot the one thing it did signify was carelessness. The bandits knew they were being pursued and either they were too stupid to realize that a gunshot could give away their position to their pursuers or more troubling still, they just didn't give a damn.

'From here on,' Johnny said presently, 'we ready ourselves for anything.'

'I was ready the moment we set out,' the kid said but it was more bravado than anything else. Though in a strange way it was true, since deep down he had been so nervous since they had set out that he was ready to clear leather at the first indication of trouble.

They rode on at a steady, though cautious pace. Here the mountains were levelling out to the West and this was the route they followed. The signs that the two bandits had been this way were plentiful in the soft ground they now travelled upon. Each side of them the mountains continued upwards but they now travelled along a valley that had been formed during prehistory, before man had even walked the planet. The valley continued on for many miles through the vast mountain range.

They had ridden on for maybe half a mile further when they spotted the Indians and fortuitously were able to scramble for cover before they were sighted. Johnny counted at least ten braves, far too many to confront and he knew that they would be foolish to engage the Indians. To do so meant certain death.

They both dismounted and quickly led their horses up a bank towards a tree-lined area where they were able to tether their horses so that they were out of view of the valley below. Then they both made their way out of the thicket until they found themselves a good vantage point. Here they could keep out of view of the trail below whilst keeping the Indians in sight.

'I guess this means our hunt is over,' Johnny said.

The kid peered over the large boulder they had hidden themselves behind and watched the Indians as they made their way along the valley. The Indians were unaware that Johnny and Wyatt were watching them and both men hoped that would remain the case.

'They sure look a bloodthirsty bunch,' the kid said, his voice little more than a whisper.

'That's a war party,' Johnny whispered back. 'See those two horses making up the remuda? I wouldn't mind betting that they previously belonged to the two bandits we've been chasing. I only got a quick glance at them back in town but them's the horses I saw.'

'Maybe,' the kid said.

'Those two horses are the only ones that are saddled,' Johnny answered. 'So I've no doubt they belonged to the two bandits.'

'You think the Indians killed them?' Wyatt asked, meaning the bandits.

Johnny nodded.

'That's a war party,' he repeated. 'They sure as hell wouldn't take prisoners and I doubt very much if our bandits simply gave those horses to the Indians. No, they're dead.'

'So what do we do now?' the kid asked, keeping his voice low. The Indians were still some way off but they were coming down the valley and would soon pass close by to where the two men were hiding.

'Let them go by,' Johnny said. 'I'm guessing the bodies of the two bandits ain't too far away. As soon as they've gone, we'll go take us a look. See what the Indians have left us.'

The kid nodded and crouched back down behind the rock. He thumbed the hammer back on his Colt, and uttered a silent prayer beneath his breath.

Johnny knew that the Indians would have taken anything of use from the two bandits. Weapons, clothing and food would come in useful to them but there was a chance that the Indians had left the money the bandits had been carrying. Most of the Indians Johnny had come across didn't fully understand the principle behind money. It meant little to them.

The two men waited while the Indians continued on a leisurely pace down the valley. Johnny was tense and half expected the Indians to notice the tracks they had left when they'd scrambled up the bank towards the tree line. There'd been no chance to cover their marks and it was likely they'd be visible to a blind man, but the Indians seemed to be oblivious to their surroundings and none of them paid much attention to the landscape around them.

Johnny looked down at the Indian party. The leader was a magnificent specimen of manhood. He sat tall in the saddle on a spectacular-looking white stallion, his proud features concentrated only on that which lay directly ahead of him. He had long flowing black hair that the low wind worried as he rode, lifting it up from the back of his shoulders so that it appeared to trail behind him. His bronze skin shone in the sunshine and there seemed to be some sort of aura surrounding him. His war party rode behind him, keeping their highly trained horses in a disciplined line.

For a moment the leader stopped, turned in his saddle to look back at his braves and Johnny felt as if his heart had jumped up into the back of his throat. He tensed and mouthed a silent prayer, thinking that if trouble started he'd take out the war chief first. That would give them their best chance against such overwhelming odds. They would have to act quickly and do as much damage as possible before the war party had a chance to react. The kid was becoming agitated too and Johnny held a hand to his own mouth, signally for the kid to remain silent.

It was a moment that seemed to stretch towards eternity before the war party once again started down the trail.

Johnny let out a sigh of relief and didn't move a muscle until the Indians had completely vanished from view.

12

The chances were that the two bandits were dead, slaughtered by the Indians. Johnny realized that, but all the same he felt a wave of disappointment when they came across the bodies of the men and his supposition was confirmed. These were the men responsible for the death of old man Walker, and Johnny had wanted to avenge that death himself. He'd gotten one of the bandits in town and the Indians had taken care of the others. That was all that really mattered but all the same Johnny felt cheated that the Indians had gotten to the men before he had.

Johnny ground tied his horse and went to examine the bodies; the kid did likewise and followed behind him. The plaintive squawk of a turkey vulture broke the silence and Johnny looked up and saw two of the scavengers circling, waiting for the meal the Indians had provided for them. He hated those birds; they reminded him of his own mortality, of how little he — or any man — really mattered. The circle of life would forever continue with or without him. One moment you're a flesh and blood man and the next you're in the belly of some damn vulture being transformed into turkey shit.

'Scavengers,' he whispered and for a moment considered letting off a shot at the birds but decided against it. All a shot would serve to do would be to startle the vultures, since they were high in the sky and well out of the range of a bullet. A sudden gunshot would also alert the Indian war party of their presence and Johnny sure didn't want to do that.

Johnny went to the dead men. The Indians hadn't mutilated them. That was still to come when the turkey vultures made use of their carcasses, but both had been relieved of their boots, hats, and gun belts. On the ground next to them were various items strewn every which way and Johnny guessed these items would be the contents of their saddlebags.

'Guess the Indians took the money,' the kid said.

Johnny nodded and then saw a single five-dollar bill among the items strewn on the ground around the two corpses. He bent and picked it up.

'All except this single Garfield,' he said and examined the bill. It was crisp, as if it had only just been minted. The bill carried the picture of James A. Garfield, the twentieth president of this great country, who had been assassinated back in 1881 after serving just twenty days in the presidential office. Johnny wondered if this was one of the very notes the bank teller had handed over to him back in Jerusalem. That seemed like a lifetime ago now.

'Can't see any more money here,' the kid said, his eyes scanning the immediate scene around them. Above them the vultures let out a shrill scream as if impatient for the two men to move on and leave them to their much-anticipated meal.

'Guess we're dealing with some mighty wealthy Indians,' Johnny said.

The kid came over to Johnny, looked down at the two dead men and shook his head.

'I thought the Indians would have scalped these fellas.' He almost sounded disappointed.

Johnny looked at the two dead men. Whilst it was true that Indians would often hand out a savage end to the white enemy, scalping had been the invention of the white man. It was a practice that the Indians had learnt from the whites and only ever carried out in retaliation of similar atrocities committed against their own people.

'Guess they figured killing them was enough,' Johnny said. He had been hoping against hope that the Indians would have left the stolen money with the dead men, finding their weapons to be of much more use, but that didn't seem to be the case. Many Indians could not see how such stuff could be more valuable than a good knife, or a gun, a tool to work the soil or a fur to keep the winter cold away.

'You intend going after those Indians?' the kid asked.

'I do,' Johnny said and then recoiled when he realized that one of the dead men was not quite as dead as they'd first assumed. The man had coughed lightly and his eyelids had flickered as a swollen tongue ran along dry lips. Johnny bent to him, grabbed him by his shoulders and lifted him gently. The bandit's throat was torn open and Johnny could see his windpipe contracting as he fought for breath, blood bubbling within the gruesome wound. The man wasn't quite dead but was sure enough getting there.

'Chasing down two bandits is one thing,' the kid, who had wandered away and was looking down into the mountains, said. He wasn't aware of the miraculous resurrection of one of the dead men.

'But a whole bunch of Indians. That ain't the same thing.'

'These men took my money,' Johnny said, feeling warm blood on his fingertips as he lifted the bandit's head slightly to try to make it a little easier for the man to breathe. 'And now those Indians have it. I want it back.'

'It ain't the same thing,' the kid said again. He sure didn't relish the prospect of chasing after those Indians. He'd never faced Indians in a fight since most of the troubles with the red men had ended years back, but he had heard stories from men who had. And if there was one thing all of those stories had in common it was the suggestion that it was best to avoid Indians if at all possible. Until today the only Indians Johnny had ever seen in the flesh had been of the tame variety, those who served as scouts on many of the cattle drives he'd been a part of but these two dead men before him were proof that these particular Indians were anything but tame.

'This man's alive,' Johnny said. 'Get me some water.'

The kid spun on his feet. At first he couldn't believe what he was seeing. He had been certain that the two bandits were dead.

'Water,' Johnny snapped as he cradled the bandit's head.

The kid immediately ran to his horse and grabbed the canteen that was hanging from the saddle.

'You figure you can just take it from those Indians?' he asked as he handed the canteen to Johnny. 'Is that what you figure?'

'Either that or die trying,' Johnny said as he unscrewed the canteen. He gently lifted it to the man's lips and poured a little into his mouth. The man swallowed but started to choke. Water spluttered over his lips and diluted the blood on his chin.

'Come on. You'll be fine,' Johnny said as he once again tilted the canteen to the bandit's lips. He knew that the man would be anything but fine, that he could pass any moment. The bandit's throat was a bloodied mess; part of an arrowhead was still embedded in the ruined flesh, and there was also a gaping wound in his chest where another arrow had found him. His injuries were too great for any chance of survival and all the bandit was doing was stubbornly hanging on to a life that would soon desert him.

The kid looked up, watching the damn turkey vultures circle while they waited for their turn to make acquaintances with the dead men.

'I hate those damn birds,' he said, echoing Johnny's feelings.

For now, though, Johnny had forgotten all about the turkey vultures and he shook the injured bandit. He knew the man had precious little time and that each and every moment could be his last. 'What happened to the money you stole? Did the Indians take it?'

The bandit's eyes opened and locked with Johnny's. He coughed again and then a smile formed on his lips as a sliver of blood trickled from the corners of his mouth. His teeth, chipped and stained as they were, looked incredibly white in contrast to the thick sheen of blood and gore that covered his mouth.

'We didn't take no money,' he laughed, then he coughed and pulled his face into a mask of agony.

'Money,' Johnny said. 'Sure there was money. You took the bank's money, you took my money.'

The man's eyes locked with Johnny's.

'No money,' he said and a moment later he was dead.

Johnny stood up, allowing the man's head to fall roughly to the ground. He took the makings from his shirt and put together a quirly. No money, he thought as he took a Lucifer to the smoke. You're telling me there's no money. The damn Indians took the money.

Wyatt took the makings from Johnny and constructed his own smoke. He had trouble with the thin rolling papers, his hands being both dirty and sweaty, but after several curses he managed to make some sort of quirly. He stuck it between his lips and leant forward, using the glowing tip of Johnny's smoke to light his own, but finding the tobacco did little to calm his frayed nerves.

'Damn,' Johnny said and removed a stray shred of tobacco from his lower lip. He rolled it between a thumb and forefinger and then flicked it on to the dead bandit. This wasn't the way things were supposed to work out.

*   *   *

The sheriff let off a shot from behind the boulder he was using for concealment and cursed when he failed to hit any of the Indians who had suddenly appeared as if from nowhere. They had come out of the darkness as though winking into existence.

'My brother,' Jim Clemens yelled and made to get up and charge the Indians but the sheriff reached out and grabbed him, pulling him back down behind the boulder.

'He's dead,' the sheriff said. 'And you'll join him if you go rushing out there.'

'We don't know that,' Clemens said. 'He could be hurt, is all.'

'Yeah we do know it,' the sheriff insisted and let off yet another wild shot. 'He took a couple of arrows and a fair few bullets and he isn't moving. I'd say that's a pretty good indication that he's dead.'

'No!' Jim yelled and before the sheriff or any of the other men could get to him he stood up and started shooting. His shots served only to spook the Indians' horses but the riders were skilled and kept their animals under control. A split second later Jim ceased shooting, ceased yelling and ceased breathing as an arrow hit him in the shoulder, spinning him around, and a bullet took off the back of his skull in a bright burst of crimson. His legs buckled and with a stunned expression on his face he fell to the ground.

'Sweet Jesus,' Walt Cartwright said.

All colour had drained from his face and he was shaking, unable to hold his own weapon steady enough for it to be of any use. He had faced battle many times during the War Between the States but that had been a long time ago and he didn't have the nerve he'd once had.

'Keep down,' the sheriff ordered. 'Keep your heads, men.'

He was now down to four men, including himself and there were ten braves attacking them. They were hopelessly outnumbered and couldn't afford to waste any more ammunition; every shot needed to count if they were to survive. The sheriff saw an opportunity to shoot as a brave passed recklessly close to the boulder and he took it. This time the bullet did some good, and tore the brave from his horse and blew his stomach open, blood immediately mixing in amongst the war paint.

'You got one.'

It had been the blacksmith who had spoken and the sheriff looked at him, speaking through gritted teeth as the Indians returned fire, sending dust into the air as their bullets chipped away at the boulder.

'Still leaves nine of the bastards,' he said. 'Though they may not be as eager to come so close next time.'

Suddenly Henry Wayne took a shot over the top of the boulder and managed to take another of the Indians out. He had been aiming at the big man on the white horse but the bullet had missed the intended target, and instead exploded into the face of another brave who had been riding close behind him. The faceless brave fell backwards from his horse and was trampled beneath the hoofs of another.

Henry whooped out in triumph and then ducked back down behind the boulder as his fire was returned.

'Correction,' the sheriff said. 'Eight of them.'

The sheriff shot again, working the lever of his Sharps rifle with more skill than he truly possessed and once again his shot found another target and yet another brave hit the ground, this time only wounded though but still out of the fight. His shoulder had been torn apart by the blast, the bone splintered and torn free of his clavicle.

'Seven,' the sheriff said, hugging the boulder while arrows and bullets whizzed above them and ricocheted off the rocks behind. He was starting to think they could maybe survive this fight after all.

And now the Indians were pulling back on the order of the brave upon the white horse. They moved back up the trail, all the while directing fire at the large boulder behind which the four white men hid.

And then there was silence.

'They've run,' the blacksmith said, hopefully.

'No,' the sheriff said, peering around the boulder. The Indians were out of view sure enough but they were still out there, the sheriff didn't doubt that. His eyes fell on the wounded Indian who he himself had shot in the shoulder. He could see the brave was breathing and although he must have been in incredible pain he was perfectly silent, lay perfectly still. The lawman felt admiration for the Indian and knew that if it had been any of his men out there, or he himself for that matter, then they would have been screaming loud enough to wake the dead.

'Brave son of a bitch,' the sheriff said. He took aim with the Sharps and shot the Indian through the head, seeing it as a mercy killing. The other Indians didn't return fire as the sheriff had hoped they would, didn't reveal their position.

'What we have here,' the sheriff said, looking at the three men, 'is a stalemate. I'm guessing those Indians are going to wait us out.'

'I can sure enough wait,' Henry Wayne said and filled the chamber in his Colt. He spun the chamber, taking comfort from the clicking sound. 'I can wait as long as it takes. I sure ain't in no hurry to go poking my head out there.'

The sheriff shook his head, thinking once again that this wasn't much of a posse. Even at full strength they hadn't been much. He cast his eyes to the body of Jim Clemens, face down in the dirt, an ugly-looking mess in the back of his head where the bullet had hit him. His brother Sam, also dead, lay out on the battlefield next to one of the fallen Indians.

'Our horses have bolted,' the sheriff said. 'We've got no food, no water. Though I don't think we'll be here long enough to starve or thirst to death.'

'You got a plan, Hoss?' Walt Cartwright, who had ridden with General Sherman during the War and believed in the wisdom of leadership, asked.

'Nope,' the sheriff said. He spat out tobacco juice and added: 'Come nightfall the Indians will attack.'

'You figure they could be trying to sneak around behind us?' the blacksmith asked, peering up at the rocks behind them. There were plenty of places for a man to hide up there and remain out of sight.

'Maybe,' the sheriff said. 'Likely that just about now those Indians are as stunned as we are. But they'll think of their next move soon enough. And we likely won't know anything about it till it happens.'

They had heard the horses approach before they had seen the Indians, which had given them a chance to take cover, but all the same the Indians had been quick to react and the gunfire that followed had spooked the horses belonging to the posse, sent them galloping off back down the trail, likely covering a goodly distance before stopping. It was a good thing that each of the posse members had the wits enough to grab their respective rifles from the saddle-boots before the horses had scattered, well all except Sam Clemens, who had no time to run before being shot down, the first slug hitting him in the leg and the second in the small of the back.

'That bluff up there,' the sheriff said

presently, pointing with his rifle. 'I reckon if one of us could get up there then we'd be in a better position to defend ourselves. The Indians are sure enough going to work their way there from the other side of the banking. Because of the banking above us we won't see them until they get there and then they'll come at us from front and back.'

'We won't have a chance if they come at us from both ends,' the blacksmith said, taking up the sheriff's train of thought.

'Which is why I'm thinking one of us should get up there before the Indians and then blast away when they show themselves.' The sheriff bit off a little more chewing tobacco.

'I could likely get up there,' Walt Cartwright said.

The sheriff admired the old man's grit but he knew that he was too slow-moving. Half of the time his legs were crippled up with arthritis, and brave man or not he was not going to be able to make the climb. As soon as the Indians realized what they were trying he would be picked off easily.

'No,' the sheriff said and then bluntly added: 'You're too old.'

'Ain't never too old,' Walt said and shook his head. 'I'm the only one of you lot seen any real action.'

'That's as maybe,' the sheriff said. 'But you're still too old. Ain't no offence meant. We all grow old.'

'I could try,' Clive Longmire, the blacksmith said. He didn't really want to but then nor did he relish the prospect of staying put and waiting for the Indians to pick them off.

The sheriff looked at him.

'Maybe you could,' the lawman said and then fell silent, once again trying to anticipate what the Indians would do next.

The way he figured it they were waiting out of view behind the banking, just far enough away to keep out of sight but close enough to know instantly when anyone made a move. This gave the Indians a double advantage over the posse. For one thing the Indians knew exactly where the four men were concealed while they themselves remained hidden, and for another they had the greater numbers.

The sheriff didn't like this situation.

Didn't like it at all.

'I'm figuring they're behind that banking,' the sheriff said, pointing to a spot ahead of them where the trail started to climb upwards into the mountains. 'If we give covering fire and you climb fast enough I figure you may just have a chance.'

'I'll do it,' the blacksmith said. 'But I'm not going to be able to defend myself till I reach the top. Can't climb and shoot so you three had better be quick on that covering fire.'

The sheriff looked at the blacksmith, thinking that with his muscular physique he may have the best chance of them all in reaching the top as quickly as possible.

'You sure?' the lawman asked.

'Sure,' the blacksmith nodded.

'Tell us when you're ready,' the sheriff said and then gave out whispered orders for the remaining two men to position themselves each side of the boulder. Meanwhile he would move about, keeping himself directly below the climbing blacksmith, which he figured would afford them the best chance of laying down effective covering fire.

The blacksmith nodded, rolled up his sleeves and slung his rifle over his shoulder, tightening the strap so it wouldn't swing about too much. It would have been easier to leave the rifle behind while he climbed, but it would become essential when he reached the top.

If he reached the top.

'I'll go now,' he said. 'Guess now is as good a time as any.'

The sheriff nodded.

'Good luck,' he said.

'Ain't luck I need,' he said. 'I need nothing short of a miracle from above.'

With that he started to climb, jumping up on to the boulder and then pulling himself up on to the jagged wall of the banking. He couldn't believe that he had made it this far, that he hadn't been immediately shot down and thinking that he might just do this, might just reach the top before the Indians even saw him, he continued to climb.

'Keep calm,' the sheriff ordered the two men with him. 'Don't shoot until you see one of the redskins.'

Suddenly one of the Indians appeared around the banking to the left of them and set off an arrow at the climbing blacksmith, but it missed and snapped against the rock face. The Indian had to disappear back behind the banking when a hail of gunfire came his way, chewing up dirt from the bank.

The blacksmith, hearing the gunshots, climbed even quicker. He had now reached the halfway point. The rest of the climb would be easier; the elevation wasn't so great and he would be able to take it at a run where previously he had been forced to remain on his hands and knees while he pulled himself from one precarious ridge to the next. He stood up and made a final run for the top of the banking and the concealment it would offer. He'd almost made it when he arched his back as an arrow thudded between his shoulder blades. The pain was incredible and the blacksmith felt as if all the force in the world had suddenly been concentrated on a single point in his back as the arrowhead tore flesh and muscle and pierced his lungs, which quickly filled with blood. The Indian who had shot the arrow had not even been seen by the men below, who could only look on in horror as the blacksmith's body first rolled and then fell, crashing to the hard rock below.

The sheriff cursed.

They were now down to three men.

13

The Indians were slowly but surely wearing them down, and the sheriff knew that it wouldn't be too long before the final attack, which he feared they had little chance of surviving. He wasn't experienced as an Indian fighter but he had heard of the Indians employing these tactics, surrounding an enemy and slowly but surely driving them crazy, not allowing them a moment to gather their thoughts or fully evaluate their situation.

He looked at the two men with him and gave a smile followed by a nod of encouragement, as if to say, 'Hold up men. We can do this. If we keep our heads we can survive this.' Deep down, though, Sheriff Hoss Banson knew that they were unlikely to survive the night. Henry looked terrified, his eyes bulging in his sockets, as if his nerves would snap at any moment. And whilst Walt

Cartwright was holding up well he was too old to be of much use. He had served bravely during the War and had a great deal of courage, but no man was immune to the passing of the years.

The sheriff shifted position to relieve a cramp and peered over the boulder, but all was quiet. The Indians were holed up behind the banking where the trail started to climb, completely concealed from view and for the last couple of hours they had been launching random attacks, a couple of braves emerging from hiding and rushing the boulder, sending hot lead into the rock and retreating before the three white men could effectively retaliate. The Indians knew they were unlikely to get any of the white men — the large boulder offered perfect cover — so the attacks were intended to demoralize the men before a more considered attack.

'It'll be dark soon,' the sheriff said and the two men with him nodded. He didn't have to say anything else and the implication in his words was clear enough.

As soon as night fell the Indians would make their move. The Indians were highly skilled fighting men and could move about as silently as a summer's breeze. Before any of the men would have any chance to react the Indians would be upon them, coming from nowhere as though appearing out of thin air. One minute there would be nothing but darkness and the next there would be a brutal attack.

'If only we had us some dynamite,' Walt said. 'I remember one time during the War when we were surrounded by a Confederate unit. There were only six of us against a full deployment of Rebs. I didn't even have a gun . . . well, I did but I had no bullets, which is the same thing. All I had was my Arkansas toothpick but one of our men had five sticks of dynamite and we blew our way through them grey coats.' He laughed at the memory and spat tobacco juice on to the ground.

The sheriff and Henry looked at the old soldier but neither of them said anything.

'Yep, if only we had us some dynamite,' the old man repeated.

'Well we ain't got none,' Henry yelled. 'If only we had us another ten men, if we had us a secret passage back to town, if we had us a gun that could shoot through rock. Trouble is we ain't got none of those things.'

'Be quiet,' the sheriff hissed, all too aware that Henry had reached the end of his tether. 'If we lose our heads now then we might just as well give up. Keep calm or we've got no chance.'

'Don't see no chance,' Henry said and then his nerve finally snapped.

He screamed, jumped up on to the boulder and set off two shots at nothing with his Sharps. His fire was immediately answered by a single shot from some concealed Indian and his chest was torn apart by the powerful 44.40 slug of a Winchester. He collapsed to his knees and then rolled back off the boulder, landing on the ground next to the sheriff. He was very much dead.

'And then there were two,' Walt said

as if this was all some sort of game. The old man wasn't shaking any more and any fear he had felt had gone. It was suddenly as if he had shed a couple of decades and he felt young, virile and totally alive.

The sheriff didn't even look at the old soldier and kept his eyes on Henry's body. He could see no hope now and for the first time in many years he looked to the Lord above for help, muttering a silent prayer beneath his breath. The lawman had never been a Godly man, but right now he felt the need to be heard by his Maker.

The situation remained static for maybe another thirty minutes and by this time it had grown dark. There was a lot of cloud in the sky and without a moon the landscape vanished around them, replaced by an inky blackness. The two men couldn't see more than a couple of feet in front of them and even then all they could make out were vague shadows, none with much substance but all of them possibly concealing the enemy.

This was it, the sheriff realized as he heard movement coming from somewhere in the darkness. He peered into the blackness, trying to make out some movement but there was nothing.

Suddenly the night air was filled with terrifying screams as the Indians yelled out a series of war chants. The chanting seemed to grow louder and louder until they were at an impossible ear-splitting volume and seemed to come from all directions, as if there were hundreds, no, thousands of Indians out there.

Walt stood up and shot blind, aiming the rifle in no particular direction but shooting off a round and hoping for blind luck.

'Come on, you sons of bitches,' he screamed and worked the lever on his rifle and fired again. The muzzle flair momentarily illuminated the scene before there was another flash and Walt was thrown backwards, a bloodied mess where his face had once been.

The sheriff was now alone.

He had twin Colts and a Sharps with

which to face off against seven blood-thirsty braves, and he knew that his chances were next to nothing. Still, he wasn't going to go down without a fight and he was determined to take as many of the Indians with him as possible before he himself was inevitably killed.

The sheriff had never been a particularly brave man but at that moment, with the hopelessness of the situation weighing down on him, he found some inner reserve of courage that he was able to draw upon.

'Come on, you redskin devils,' the sheriff muttered. That he would die tonight was pretty much a given and perhaps because of this realization, because he had nothing to lose, he felt a fury deep within himself that he had never experienced before. Each second of life became precious and he would fight to the very end. As long as there was a single breath left in his lungs he would fight with a ferociousness he had never before felt.

Deciding that he had nothing to lose

by changing position, he took a deep breath and prepared to move. If he couldn't see the Indians in this damn dark then it was a good chance that they couldn't see him. If he could move from behind the boulder then maybe it would confuse the Indians, give him a few more precious seconds of life. He lay down on the ground and, Colt in one hand, rifle strapped over his shoulder, he started sliding out from his concealment. He had just cleared the boulder when he saw movement directly ahead of him, little more than a shadow, an almost imperceptible shifting of black on black.

He calmly levelled the Colt and fired. The powder flash was momentarily brilliant and the sheriff saw that his shot had struck home as the agonized features of an Indian were lit up. Then the darkness returned and the sheriff heard the Indian fall to the ground, closely followed by even more chanting and screaming, this time with a greater fury. Several shots sounded and the ground around the sheriff puffed up as bullets tore into the dirt, but miraculously he wasn't hit.

The sheriff shot back, guessing where to aim and then scrambled towards the banking where earlier the Indians had hidden. He heard another shot then, and then another and this time the shooting was coming from behind and above him and for a moment he figured that a couple of Indians had scaled the rocks and were even now waiting for the opportunity to pick him off, but he soon realized that this was not the case and he heard the Indians returning fire.

The sheriff managed to reach another boulder, smaller this time but large enough for him to hide behind. He sat there, confused. There seemed to be a full-scale battle going on and gunfire sounded from all directions. Someone was shooting from the rocks above and the Indians were returning fire, and all the lawman was able to make out during the brief flashes of brilliance that followed each shot was that he was no longer alone in facing the Indians.

Someone had come to his aid.

'Jerusalem,' the sheriff said as he realized just who that someone was. It had to be Johnny Jerusalem, and by the sound of the gunfire Jerusalem wasn't alone.

'The kid,' the sheriff realized. 'That damn kid.' Jerusalem had the kid with him. It had to be, it was the only thing that made any sense and this gave the sheriff a new impetus. He took up his Sharps and started firing into the darkness, guessing the position of the Indians.

Things continued like this for several moments before the sheriff heard the sound of horses and realized the Indians were retreating. They would have no idea who the newcomers were, indeed how many there were, and had decided that the odds had changed significantly.

'Sheriff?' a voice yelled out as the sound of the galloping ponies faded into the distance.

Banson licked his dry lips and smiled. The shout confirmed that it was Jerusalem out there in the darkness. The lawman recognized the voice.

'Yeah,' he yelled back, He couldn't believe that he had survived this. He felt light headed.

'How many men you got down there?'

'Just me,' the sheriff said and stood up. 'I'm all that's left.'

For a moment there was silence before Johnny answered.

'Hold your fire. We're coming down to you.'

14

'So what do we do now?' the sheriff asked. He was sucking on a quirly and watching as the kid set about making a small fire. The three men had decided to wait until first light before moving on back down out of the mountains. It was safer that way, Johnny had insisted, if they didn't want to ride straight into what was left of the war party.

'It'll be too soon if I never see an Indian again,' the sheriff said. He had a charley horse from crouching so long behind the boulder and he tried to massage feeling back into the cramped muscle.

Johnny had told the sheriff what had happened to the two bandits they had been pursuing, of how he and the kid and come upon their bodies only after narrowly avoiding a confrontation with the war party themselves. How the two bandits had been stripped of their weapons as well as the money they had stolen from the bank, which included Johnny's seven hundred and fifty dollars.

The way Johnny told it was that he and the kid had been in pursuit of the war party, determined to ambush them and recover the town's money. They had been riding through the day and kept going well into nightfall when they had heard the gunfire, and figuring that that meant the posse had engaged the war party in battle they had gotten there as quickly as they could. The sheriff was sure glad of that. The lawman knew that without the intervention of Johnny and the kid the Indians would have surely killed him, just as they had killed the rest of his posse.

'Then I guess it's all over,' the sheriff said after a moment of silence during which the three men drank the coffee the kid had boiled up in the old pot they carried.

'Don't know about that,' Johnny said.

148

The sheriff shook his head; he for one was tired of the chase. 'We need to get back to town. Make arrangements for the bodies of my men to be collected so they get a decent burial.'

'We could cover the bodies,' the kid suggested. 'Protect them from most of the critters.'

'It's a three-day ride back to town,' Johnny said. 'And three days back again. Critters or no critters these men won't look too pretty in six days. If they've got to be buried then here is as good a place as any.'

'We ain't leaving them here,' the sheriff said.

'Well I sure ain't carrying no dead man,' Johnny said.

The kid shivered at the thought.

'Me neither,' he said.

'Our horses scattered when the Indians attacked,' the sheriff said. 'Maybe come first light we can round them up and take the bodies back with us.'

'Maybe,' Johnny said and then added, unaware of how insensitive he sounded

149

to the fate of the posse members: 'I sure do hate to lose my money. It's all I've got in the world.'

'You got a whole lot more than these men here,' the kid said, pointing to the row of dead men.

'And that ain't much,' Johnny retorted and spat into the dirt.

'There ain't much chance of catching up with that war party anyways,' the sheriff said. 'They'll be long gone by dawn.'

'They'll likely use that money to buy weapons and whiskey and then go on the warpath again,' said Johnny, then tossed the remains of his own quirly into the fire. He took the coffee pot from the fire, using a folded glove to protect his hand, and poured himself another cup of the thick liquid.

'All I know is we ain't going to catch them now,' the sheriff said.

Johnny nodded.

He had hoped to have taken the Indians by surprise, sneak up on them before they were even aware of his existence. That way he would have had a chance of spooking their horses, scattering them, picking several of the Indians off from concealment, chasing the others away and getting his money back. That had been a slim chance at best but now, with all that had happened, there was no chance.

'Guess it just ain't worth it,' the kid said, looking at the bodies on the ground.

They had dragged the bodies of the posse members from where they had fallen and positioned them on the ground next to the large boulder that had served to protect them from the Indians. Johnny had covered them with the blankets he and the kid carried in their saddle-bags. They had left the bodies of the Indians where they had fallen, figuring the critters could take their fill.

The sheriff looked at the kid, his youthful face illuminated by the flickering of the fire; at that moment the kid looked as if he had aged ten years since he'd first seen him in town.

'You got that right,' the sheriff said.

'Next to losing these men the loss of the bank's money don't seem at all important.'

Johnny said nothing about that but the expression upon his face suggested that he didn't fully agree with the sheriff. His piece of the missing money was mighty important to him. The way the sheriff was acting, though, convinced Johnny that he had been wrong about him, that the lawman hadn't been involved in the bank robbery after all. If he had then the death of the two bandits may have suited him but he surely wouldn't have given up on the money so easily.

For several moments the three men were silent. They all sat there, staring into the fire, watching the flames dance, each lost in private thoughts. They were exhausted, and top of all that the sheriff just couldn't seem to shift his charley horse. Sleep would have come so easily to any one of them, but none would allow themselves that luxury tonight. The chances were that the Indian war party had long gone by now, likely put a couple of miles behind them. But there was no guarantee that the Indians hadn't decided to sneak back and find out just how many men had come to the aid of the sheriff.

It was Johnny who eventually broke the silence.

'First light,' he said. 'We start back to town.'

He wasn't going to get any argument from the other two men.

15

As it turned out they had been able to locate two of the scattered horses. The Indians had likely rounded up the others but these two had wandered into the mountains. It was the kid who had spotted them foraging amongst the undergrowth. They had then draped their dead over one of the horses, carefully tying the corpses in place, while the sheriff claimed the remaining horse. Once that was done they made their way down out of the mountains.

They rode slowly, each of them weary in the saddle but keeping their wits about them, alert and ready should the war party put in another appearance but as each hour passed without incident they began to relax. Sometime after noon they stopped to eat and whilst the kid set about making a fire, Johnny took some beans, jerky and coffee from his saddle-bags.

They ate their meal in silence. Johnny kept turning the bandit's last words over and over in his mind.

We didn't take no money. No money. No money.

What had that meant? Had the bandit been mocking them, telling them that there was no longer any money since the Indian war party had taken it or had he meant something else entirely? It seemed a strange thing to say.

We didn't take no money. No money. No money.

Whatever the bandit had meant with his dying words the fact remained that they had been riding for days in pursuit of the two bandits and after all this the money had gone.

'I'd be mighty obliged if one of you would loan me your makings,' the sheriff said as he drained the last of his coffee. 'Smoked all mine.'

The kid handed his own makings across to the lawman.

'We should get going,' Johnny said

after swallowing the last of his meal. 'Ain't no good staying here too long. The Indians will be long gone by now but I wouldn't rule out them turning back and attacking us when we're unprepared.'

He used a handful of foliage to wipe clean his tin plate and returned it to his saddle-bags before climbing into the saddle. They then rode on in silence and didn't stop until night had once again fallen. They made camp in a wooded area, knowing that by noon tomorrow they would have come out of the mountains and would reach Jerusalem after another day. The Indian threat had lessened somewhat but the three men didn't feel confident enough not to set a guard on the camp. It was decided that each of them would stand guard for an hour or so while the others slept. It was Johnny himself who drew first watch and leaving the other two men to bed down beside the fire he went and found a suitable rock to sit on while he listened to the sounds of the night.

Sometime later the wind picked up and Johnny cursed, lifted his collars up and pulled his hat down over his face, and not long after that it started to rain. At first it was nothing more than a trickle but gradually it picked up and became a fierce storm, causing the men to abandon their camp and carefully lead their horses down the trail, looking for somewhere to take shelter.

They were cold, tired and miserable, and the wind only served to make them feel worse by driving the stinging rain into them.

It was as if nature itself was mocking them.

★   ★   ★

Three days later they arrived in Jerusalem and as they rode down the dusty main street, Johnny suddenly felt excited at the prospect of seeing Cherry Mewis again. He had originally intended to head straight back to the ranch house but the sheriff had insisted he and the kid accompanied him into town. They had the bodies of the posse with them and the lawman felt it would show more respect if they all rode into town together, if they were all there to explain to the town's people that they had failed to recover the stolen money and had lost a lot of good men in the process.

There was also the matter, the sheriff pointed out, of paperwork that would have to be done. Reports had to be filled out and he would need both Johnny and the kid's signatures on those reports. The bandits had stolen a considerable sum of government money from the town bank, which meant that nothing could be overlooked as far as the official paperwork was concerned. The lawman intended to inform the army of the Indian war party and hope that they would send out a unit to confront the Indians, force them back to the reservation. It wasn't that the sheriff didn't have any sympathy with the plight of the Indians but at the moment, with his own men dead, all he cared about was answering the war cries of the Indians with a brutal and terrible force.

'The town ain't woken yet,' Johnny observed as they rode down Main Street, their horses trampling the remnants of the dawn dew into the ground. He suddenly felt incredibly weary and the stubble upon his face, now qualifying as a beard, felt heavy being caked with dirt and sweat as it was. Maybe it would be better if he didn't run into Miss Mewis until he'd had a chance to wash up some.

'I'm dog tired,' he remarked.

'I think I could sleep for a month myself,' the kid said. He had several days of fine stubble on his youthful face and a heck of a lot of trail grime on his clothes and in his hair.

'Plenty of time to sleep later,' the sheriff said and glanced back at the horse trailing behind them, his eyes falling to the bodies of his men. From now until eternity those men would do nothing but sleep.

They rode directly to the undertaker's where the sheriff dismounted and rapped on the heavy door with the butt of a Colt.

A moment later the undertaker's cadaverous face, sleepy-eyed and tousled-haired, appeared in the doorway. He looked at the sheriff and then his gaze flittered moth-like over Johnny and the kid before resting on the dead posse men.

'Oh my,' he said.

'Timmons,' the sheriff said, 'get these men ready for the afterlife. I want the full service, no expense spared. You can bill the town. I authorize it.'

The undertaker's eyes lit up. The full service, the sheriff had said. No expense spared, which would prove mighty lucrative, and he had several deluxe caskets in his workshop that were ready to go. Just lately, with times the way they were, folks weren't requesting the deluxe service for their dearly beloved.

'Yes sir,' he said and scuttled over to the horse that carried the dead men. He ran his tongue over his upper lip while he regarded the corpses with something akin to delight.

'Knock yourself out,' Johnny remarked bitterly. He had come up against some bad men in his time but none of them had given him such a feeling of revulsion as he experienced here and now with this morbid, scrawny bag of bones who was the town undertaker. Timmons, perhaps recalling the way Johnny had manhandled him on the morning of the bank robbery, said nothing in reply.

The sheriff nodded and rode across the street towards his own office, Johnny and the kid following closely behind.

'I'll get us some coffee going,' the sheriff said as he tethered his horse to the hitching rail outside his office. 'And I'll send over to the saloon to get us some bacon and eggs brought over. No need to start filling out reports on an empty stomach.'

'That sounds mighty good to me,' Johnny said and climbed out of his own saddle. There wasn't a square inch of his body that didn't seem to ache but these pains were secondary to the rumblings in his belly. He hitched his horse alongside the sheriff's. 'Right about now I could sure do with a meal.'

The kid nodded and dismounted. 'If I ever get to eating, I don't think I'll ever stop,' he said.

Weary, hungry and cold the three men walked into the sheriff's office.

16

'Damn, that was good,' Johnny said as he mopped the last of the gravy from his plate with a piece of bread. 'Likely the best meal I've ever eaten.'

The sheriff leaned over, his chair creaking in protest, and slid open the top drawer of his desk. He pulled out a box of thin cigars and placed one between his teeth. He offered the box and both Johnny and the kid took one each.

'Obliged,' Johnny said bringing a match to the cigar. He sucked in the thick smoke and allowed it to circle around his mouth before pushing it out between his teeth. Banson wasn't such a bad sort, after all, Johnny reflected as he drew in the creamy smoke. He had started out after the bandits with the conviction that the sheriff was somehow involved in the robbery, but now he found he was developing a respect for the lawman.

We didn't take no money. No money. No money.

The office door swung open and a redheaded kid stuck his head around the doorway.

'Town council want to see you, Sheriff,' the kid said.

'Tell them I'll be along presently,' the sheriff snapped and just as the kid was about to vanish he called him back. 'Lurch,' he said, 'before you report to the council, take our horses over to the livery stable and see that they're fed, watered and brushed down.' The lawman reached into his pocket and tossed a coin over to the kid, which the kid caught in his right hand.

'Sure thing, Sheriff.'

The sheriff nodded and smiled when the kid closed the office door.

'I may have ridden myself down to the bone,' the lawman said, 'but that don't cut nothing with the town council. They expect me to carry out my official duties no matter what. I'll finish my smoke first, though. Won't hurt them fellas none to wait a little.' He took another long draw on his cigar.

The three men smoked in silence for several moments before the sheriff again reached into his drawer and pulled out a thick ledger.

'Damn paperwork,' he said. 'It's the last thing I want to deal with at the moment and I guess you fellas feel the same.'

Johnny and the kid exchanged a glance, nodded.

'Best done when the mind is fresh, though.' The sheriff gave the other two men an apologetic smile.

More than two hours had passed before they were done and the sheriff told Johnny and the kid that they were free to go. The lawman had written out a statement for each of them, and had also drafted out a telegram, which he would later send to the army. The problem of the rogue Indians was a military one now and it was they who would be responsible for recovering the large amount of stolen government money. There was little chance of the money ever being recovered, though. They all knew that, which was why the sheriff was so diligent in obtaining signed statements from the two men. The lawman was under no illusion that some would blame him for the robbery, for allowing it to happen in his town in the first place. The old ways were fast vanishing; bank robbers couldn't ride the plains with impunity any longer and lawmen had to be up to the task of keeping the peace in a fast modernizing West.

Immediately after leaving the sheriff's office Johnny and the kid crossed the street to collect their horses from the livery stable. The boy the sheriff had called Lurch had done what he had been told and the horses had been fed, watered, and brushed down.

'Obliged,' Johnny said, realizing that he had no money to offer the owner of the livery stable. 'Guess the sheriff will take care of all costs.'

The livery stable man nodded and smiled, revealing a row of chipped, tobacco-stained teeth. He handed the reins over to Johnny and then went and collected the kid's horse.

'Sorry you didn't get those bandits,' the livery stable owner said as he handed the reins of his horse to the kid.

'Obliged,' the kid said as he mounted up. He too had no money to offer the man and so he followed Johnny out of the stable and into the now bright daylight. The street was surprisingly empty but both Johnny and the kid were aware of eyes upon them as they rode out of town.

Neither of them looked back.

With food in their bellies they were both feeling a little better, though they rode in total silence. Each of them carried the strains and aches of the long ride they had endured, a long ride, which had turned out to have been for nothing, and there was nothing to say and so they rode side by side, following the trail that led to Johnny's place. There might just as well have been a million miles between them for each was only vaguely aware of the other man as they rode.

We didn't take no money. No money. No money.

The loss of the money was still playing on Johnny's mind, but he kept telling himself that it could have been a whole lot worse. He may have lost every cent he owned in the world, but he still had his life unlike old man Jessie Walker as well as the men who had made up the sheriff's posse. When you looked at things that way the money didn't seem all that important. And besides, Johnny figured, he still had the ranch and with a little hard work he could make a good life here — that would be the way to honour both the memory of the man who had been a father to him, as well as that of old man Walker.

We didn't take no money. No money. No money.

The dying bandit's words popped once more into Johnny's mind, continuing to torment him. It seemed a strange

168

thing for the bandit to have said. Not that the Indians had taken the money but that there hadn't been any money. Of course, the man was dying at the time, likely in a shock and Johnny would have dismissed it completely out of hand were it not for something Cherry Mewis had said when this had all started.

She had told Johnny that the bank had been holding an unusually large amount of money, that the bandits had been incredibly fortuitous in staging their robbery when they had. The sheriff had been one of the few who had known of the money, which was why Johnny had set out after the bandits without waiting for the lawman and his posse. Johnny was originally convinced that the sheriff had been involved in the robbery, that he was deliberately allowing the bandits to make good their escape and that he would later collect his cut of the proceedings. Now, though, Johnny felt that he had been allowing his past experiences with

Banson to colour his view; there was no way the lawman was involved in the robbery. Johnny was sure of that and if indeed there had been an inside man, someone who had tipped the bandits off, then it certainly wasn't Sheriff Hoss Banson. The fact he had immediately jumped to the conclusion that the sheriff was involved meant that he had missed something.

He was still missing something.

Too late now, Johnny thought. The money was gone, most likely the Indians had it, which meant that soon it would end up with some unscrupulous dealer for a couple of crates of rifles and a whole lot of whiskey.

There was no money.

'Damn,' Johnny spat and reached into his shirt for his makings. He quickly put a smoke together and tossed the makings across to the kid.

The kid caught the leather pouch, nodded his thanks.

'We'll get back to the ranch and rest the horses for a few days,' Johnny said.

'Then we'll ride out and round us up some mavericks. Sooner I start the ranch working the better.'

The kid nodded and the rest of the ride was spent in silence.

17

Two days later Johnny decided it was time to take a ride back to town to see if he could extend his credit at the general store in order to obtain provisions for the trip he had planned. There were mavericks aplenty in the mountains around Jerusalem and Johnny planned on roping in a herd sooner rather than later.

They had spent the last couple of days repairing the fences around the corral and Johnny was pleased with the results. The kid was a fine worker, skilled as a ranch-hand, and together the two of them had the ranch looking better than it had for a long time. They were now ready to bring in their first herd, and the sooner they got out into the mountains and rounded up the horses the better. Winter was not too far away and bringing in a herd of wild horses would be a difficult enough task without unpredictable weather making it worse.

'Guess I'll have to think of a brand,' Johnny said as they reached the out-skirts of Jerusalem. Ahead of them the roofs of the building were gleaming in the afternoon sunlight.

The kid nodded, gave a slight smile but said nothing.

'JJ,' Johnny said. 'Johnny Jerusalem. Likely someone's already registered that brand, though.'

'Maybe,' the kid said.

' 'Course,' Johnny continued, 'I could put a double J with a circle around it or put it inside a triangle. I'm not sure how the rules work when you register a brand but I guess I'll soon find out.'

'Guess you will,' the kid said and Johnny smiled. The kid was not what one could call the talkative kind, but that suited Johnny fine since he could talk up a storm all by his lonesome. This made the kid the perfect compan-ion and they said nary a word to each other until they had ridden into town.

If Johnny had any concerns about his

credit in the store then they were soon dispelled when the storekeeper, Whitey, pumped Johnny's hand and told him to take what he needed.

'Once again I'm obliged to you,' Johnny said and handed over the list he had drawn up before leaving the ranch.

The storekeeper examined the note and then smiled. He immediately started pottering about the store, putting the requested provisions on to the long counter that ran the length of the store.

'I'll come back in thirty minutes,' Johnny said and when the storekeeper nodded he stepped back out into the afternoon sunshine. The street was busy now, people going every which way as they went about their business and, feeling foolish, like a lovesick child, Johnny looked up and down the street in the hope of spotting Cherry Lee Mewis. She was nowhere to be seen but Johnny did notice the kid talking to Sheriff Banson.

'Howdy,' Johnny said as he approached them.

Banson looked at Johnny, offered the

slimmest of smiles. 'Kid tells me you're riding out into the mountains in search of mavericks,' he said. 'I wish you luck with that.'

'Obliged,' Johnny said. He knew that he and Banson would never be real friends, not with their history, but he certainly felt a new-found respect for the lawman. Those nights out on the trail in pursuit of the bandits and then the renegade Indians had given Johnny a new understanding of the man. He didn't think Banson would ever be a first-class lawman but he guessed the man was doing his best, and there was a lot to be said for that.

'Don't think you'll have to worry none about Indians,' the sheriff said. 'Last I heard the army were chasing them across the territory.'

'That's good to know,' the kid said and looked at Johnny, who remained impassive, said nothing.

'I'll stand you fellas a drink,' the sheriff said. 'I need to talk to you both in any case.'

'You've recovered my money?' Johnny asked, though he knew that wouldn't be the case.

'Not one single cent,' the sheriff said. 'Let's get that drink.'

Johnny nodded, joked: 'Drown my sorrows in a bottle.'

The three men crossed the street and went into the Indian Creek.

It turned out that the sheriff stood both Johnny and the kid a couple of drinks. While they drank the sheriff told them that the army had sent a patrol out to confront the Indian war party, but that there wasn't much hope in finding them since the Indians would have been long gone by now, taking with them all hope of ever recovering the bank's money. The latest report was that the army had confronted a party of warring Indians along the Candlefall Ridge, but that the Indians had fled after a brief fight. The men who had stolen the money from the bank were dead, and that, as far as the sheriff was concerned, was pretty much the end of the matter.

'You've not come out of it entirely penniless, though,' the sheriff concluded and handed both men a crisp new ten-dollar note, which he pulled from his breast pocket.

Johnny looked at the money, frowned.

'Town council always pays posse members ten dollars a piece,' the sheriff explained. 'You two qualify for the payment. I was going to ride out to your spread later today with the money but you've saved me the trip.'

'Always happy to help out the law,' Johnny said and bought the next round of beers himself. It would be the last drink, he decided, since he and the kid were riding for the mountains come morning and clear heads were pretty much a necessity.

*　*　*

Cherry Mewis had been alone in the bank when the woman came in. Mr Carver was out of town, was not due back until later that morning, and Cherry had found herself with the task of running things in his stead. One of the clerks would be in around eleven but until then Cherry was on her own, not that it mattered since the morning had been quiet and this woman was the first customer to put in an appearance since Cherry had opened up for business.

'I'd like to see Mr Carver, please,' the woman said. She sounded nervous, her voice frayed around the edges. Her eyes were frightened and darted about in her head.

'Mr Carver's out of town,' Cherry said.

'When will he be back?' the woman asked, now seeming more nervous than ever.

'Later,' Cherry said. 'I'm in charge for the moment. I'm sure I can help you.'

'No,' the woman said. 'I need to see Mr Carver.'

18

An hour later, Johnny and the kid had collected their provisions from the general store, loaded them on their horses and were just about to ride out of town when Johnny heard someone calling his name. He spun on his feet and saw Cherry Mewis waving to him from the end of the street. She was standing with another woman, a woman Johnny didn't recognize, and they both started across the street towards him.

Johnny and the kid exchanged puzzled glances as the two women approached.

'This is Elle Carlton,' Cherry said by way of introduction, though the name meant nothing to Johnny or the kid and again the two men exchanged puzzled glances. Johnny searched his memory, thinking the woman may have been someone he'd known way back when, but neither the name nor the face meant anything to him. 'Pleased to make your acquaintance,' he said, fully expecting the woman to accuse him of forgetting her.

'She came into town looking for her husband,' Cherry said and then to the woman: 'Show them the photograph.'

The woman reached into the velvet bag she carried and pulled out a small sepia photograph. She handed it to Johnny.

Johnny took the photograph and looked at an image of a man standing beside a handsome-looking horse. The man was smartly dressed with a derby hat perched at a jaunty angle upon his head.

'It was taken last year,' the woman said. 'Things were good then. Before Clem lost everything we had. The bank was threatening to foreclose on us, take our property and stock, which is why Clem got himself involved in all this. Clem wasn't a bad man.' Her eyes started to fill with tears.

'This man,' Johnny said and looked at Cherry Mewis, who responded with a nod of her head. Johnny recognized the man. He was one of the bandits who had held up the town bank.

'Elle's husband,' Cherry said. 'She came into town looking for him. She knows he's dead now, I gave her the bad news.'

'He wasn't a bad man,' the woman repeated as she fought back the sobs that rattled in her throat.

'He was with a bunch of men who robbed a bank,' Johnny said, bluntly. 'A good man was killed in that robbery and several more good men during the pursuit of your husband and the other man.'

'No one was supposed to get hurt,' the woman said. Her emotions finally got the better of her and she started to openly cry, which prompted Cherry to place a comforting arm around her.

'If Clem had known it would go off like this he never would have gotten involved. I begged him not to do it but he told me everything would be all right. That nothing could go wrong and besides, it wasn't really a robbery.'

'Wasn't a robbery?' Johnny looked the woman directly in the eye. It was difficult for him to feel any sympathy for her and as far as he was concerned the bandits had gotten what they deserved. No amount of tears was going to bring old man Walker back, or Johnny's money for that matter.

'That wasn't supposed to happen,' the woman said. 'Clem was promised that wouldn't happen.'

Johnny was completely lost now. He didn't have any idea what the damn fool woman was talking about.

'We're going to the sheriff,' Cherry said. 'I thought you might like to hear just what Elle's got to say.'

Johnny handed the photograph back to the woman.

'You've got that right,' he said and he and the kid accompanied the two women across the street to the sheriff's office. The lawman's horse was tethered to the hitching rail outside the office and the kid patted it gently before following the others inside.

* * *

'Carver,' Johnny spat the name and placed the freshly rolled quirly in his mouth and took a match to it. 'Son of a bitch.' Everything made sense now. That's what the dying man had meant.

There was no money. No money. No money.

'That son of a bitch,' Johnny said and turned to leave the sheriff's office but the lawman called him back.

'That's a mighty fine story,' he said. 'But it don't prove anything and I want solid evidence before going up against a man like Thomas J. Carver.'

'It's enough for me,' Johnny said, leaning forward and resting his knuckles on the edge of the sheriff's desk. 'I had a suspicion there was something odd about this robbery right from the off. There was a lot of money in the bank, by all accounts an unusually large amount for this town.'

'That much is true,' the sheriff said. 'Ordinarily the bank wouldn't have been worth holding up and yet it was hit at the only time the safe was full.'

'Not many people knew that about that money,' Johnny said. 'With everything we've been told here today I'd say it was pretty clear that the bank manager himself was behind it.'

'Ain't clear enough,' Banson said.

'When we came across the bandits in the mountains one of them was still alive,' Johnny started but paused when he caught the eye of Elle Carlton. The story he was about to tell the sheriff concerned her husband's dying words and he didn't figure the woman needed to hear it. He looked at Cherry and smiled.

Cherry, getting his meaning perfectly, took Elle by the arm.

'Maybe we should leave the men to it,' she said and led the other woman outside.

Johnny and the sheriff locked eyes while the kid gave nervous glances around the office, as though contemplating leaving with the women.

The way Elle Carlton had told it was like this:

'*My husband wasn't no bank robber.*' She had said it with conviction. He was a farmer and didn't know one end of a gun from the other. The other men with him were the same, none of them would have ever attempted hitting a bank but then this wasn't any ordinary robbery. Not really a robbery at all, Carlton had told his wife.

It had started more than a year ago when the Carltons, who owned a small farm in Dalton, had found themselves facing particularly hard times. There had been one too many bad winters and the farmland had yet again failed to yield any useable crops. This was hard enough but the livestock had fallen foul of disease, which proved to be the final blow for the Carltons. They had gone in the space of only a few years from running a small but prosperous farm to trying to manage a ruinous money pit. Eventually the bank started closing in. The Carltons had secured a loan several years back in order to purchase more land and extend the farm. It had seemed a good idea at the time; the farm was making money and the extra land would allow them to make yet more money. Clem Carlton had visions of creating an agricultural empire in the Midwest but instead it had all turned into a nightmare.

That was where Carver came in. The bank manager knew the Carltons were in trouble — he was intimate with their bank accounts. He had offered them a life line, a chance to wipe out their debts and make enough money besides to start up a new farm somewhere else, somewhere where the conditions were far more favourable. The men were just supposed to bust into the bank; they wouldn't really take any money since Carver would have already removed the money, hidden it somewhere else to divide up later.

We didn't take no money. No money. No money.

'There ain't no proof against Carver,'

the sheriff said. 'Only the word of this woman. Mr Carver's well respected in this town and this woman is the wife of one of the men who held up the bank. No jury will believe her and I could lose my job if I make a move on someone like Carver with only her say so.'

'She's telling the truth,' Johnny said.

'And on what basis to you make that assumption?' the lawman asked. He took a cigar from the box on his desk but this time didn't offer one to Johnny or the kid.

Johnny thought back to the day of the bank robbery. It all made perfect sense to him and he didn't have a single doubt that the woman had been telling the truth, that her husband and his friends had been part of some sort of conspiracy engineered by the bank manager. The way it had happened backed all this up. The bandits had seemed like amateurs simply because that's what they were. They had ordered everyone in the bank, everyone except the bank manager, to lay down face first on the floor.

Sure, they had tossed a sack to the bank manager but no one had seen any actual money being placed into that sack. It was likely that all the bandits had left that bank with had been a sack of paper and Johnny's own seven hundred and fifty dollars. By that point Johnny had been unconscious and he had no idea what had happened after that. The next thing he had known the bandits had fled the bank and the shoot-out had started.

'I know that woman's telling the truth,' he repeated.

'Well it ain't enough,' the sheriff said, stubbornly.

'Damn,' Johnny raised his voice and glared at the sheriff. 'If you don't go after Carver then I will.'

'Then I'll be forced to arrest you,' the sheriff said.

A silence fell and the kid, feeling increasingly uneasy, made his way to the door. His hand paused on the handle for a moment before he opened the door and went outside, figuring he'd leave the two men to it.

Johnny watched the kid go and then turned back to the sheriff. Without being invited to do so he slid a stool from beneath the sheriff's desk and sat down.

'I'm telling you Carver's involved,' he growled.

The sheriff sighed and then slid the box of cigars across to Johnny and smiled when the man took one. He tossed a box of Lucifers on to the desk.

'That may be so,' he said, 'but I'm a lawman, I'm paid to look after this town and I can't go after a respected citizen with nothing more than the word of a bandit's wife to back me up. Surely, you can see that.'

Johnny nodded. He guessed he could, but all the same he was convinced that the bank manager was behind all this. If that was so then it meant that not only was there a possibility of getting the town's money back, but his own seven hundred and fifty dollars too. And of course there was also the fact that if the woman's story was true then Carver

189

was as much responsible for the death of old man Walker as the man who had pulled the trigger. The posse members too, the bank manager would also have their blood on his hands.

'Guess I'll have to find more proof, then,' he said.

'You bring me solid evidence,' the sheriff said, 'and I'll throw Carver behind bars myself.'

It was then that a gunshot sounded outside.

It was followed by a piercing scream.

19

Johnny and the sheriff were both holding iron as they came out on to the street, neither of them knowing what to expect. They were acting on instinct and kept low as they went out into the afternoon sunshine.

They were stopped dead in their tracks by the scene before them.

The woman, Mrs Carlton, lay on the ground, very much dead, the front of her dress stained by blood, her blood. The kid stood over the woman, his gun in his hand and aimed at Carver. The kid dared not take a shot at the bank manager else he hit Cherry Mewis. Carver held Miss Mewis, an arm around her neck while his free hand held a Navy Colt.

Johnny looked at the scene before them and then turned to the sheriff.

'Is that proof enough for you?' he

asked, a bad attempt at black humour.

'That'll pretty much do it,' the sheriff said.

'Don't any of you try anything,' the bank manager yelled and started backing away, dragging Cherry with him. 'One wrong move and I'll shoot Miss Mewis.'

There was panic in his voice, which Johnny didn't like. He had seen men in this state before and knew that the man would be apt to snap at any moment, perhaps even pulling the trigger by accident, an involuntary twitch which would prove deadly for Cherry Mewis. He holstered his own gun, held out his hands, willing the bank manager to remain in control, and took a step forward.

'Keep calm,' he said. 'Everyone keep calm.' His eyes went to Cherry, whose eyes were bulging in terror. The bank manager held her tightly, her neck trapped in the crook of his arm. His other arm held the pistol against Cherry's temple. If he pulled the trigger then the woman would have no chance. The .36 calibre bullet would likely tear the top of her head clean off at such close range.

'Let's just keep this under control,' the lawman said and holstered his own weapon.

Only the kid now had his weapon aimed at the bank manager, who was backing slowly away from them and he too lowered his weapon. He looked at Johnny and the sheriff, unsure what to do.

'Don't anyone try and stop me,' the bank manager shouted. 'One sudden move and I'll pull the trigger.' For a moment Cherry struggled against his hold but he pushed the pistol a little harder, reminding her of its presence. She ceased fighting, took great care to step backwards in perfect rhythm with Carver. If they so much as stumbled then the gun was likely to go off.

'He came across the street,' the kid said and his eyes fell to the dead woman. 'She went to confront him as soon as she spotted him; there was no holding her back. Before anyone could react Carver shot her in the belly. He killed her.'

'I didn't want to do that,' Carver shouted and took another step backwards. 'She came at me like a harridan. She went berserk.'

'She blamed you for the death of her husband,' Johnny said. 'Guess you can't blame her for that.'

'I didn't kill her husband,' Carver said.

'That's true,' Johnny said. 'The Indians did that, but it was you that put him in that situation.'

'I didn't kill her husband,' Carver repeated.

'Don't matter who killed him,' Johnny retorted. 'You set up that bank robbery, kicked off the chain of events that's culminated here today in you shooting that woman dead.'

'I killed the woman,' Carver said, as if he couldn't quite believe it. For a moment he seemed confused, as if not knowing where he was but then he tightened his grip on Cherry Mewis, pulling her closer to him. 'I'll kill Miss Mewis too if anyone tries anything.'

'You don't want to hurt anyone else,' the sheriff said. 'Put down your gun, let Miss Mewis go.'

For a moment it looked as if the bank manager was going to comply with the sheriff's order. He stood still for a moment, but didn't relax his grip on the woman. If anything his grip tightened even further.

'I'll hang for this,' Carver said.

'You hurt Miss Mewis and the rope'll be the least of your worries,' Johnny warned, which earned him a look of reproach from the sheriff.

'Just relax,' the lawman said. 'Let's keep calm. No one else needs get hurt.'

Carver backed away a little more, almost having to drag the woman with him.

'Put the gun down,' the sheriff commanded, keeping his tone low but firm. 'You can't get away. Let the woman go and I'll speak to the judge for you, fix it so you go to jail rather than hang.'

Carver looked at the sheriff.

'You can do that?' he asked.

'It's your only chance now,' the lawman said. 'I know you're not really a killer and I'll speak up for you.'

Carver nodded but still he did not release the woman.

'First you must leave Miss Mewis go. Let her go and put the gun down.' The sheriff held his own hands up where they were visible, palms facing the gunman.

'Best listen to him,' Johnny said. 'Put the gun down.'

A crowd had gathered, attracted by the sound of gunfire. They lined each side of the street, watching the scene before them as if it was a great entertainment rather than a life or death situation. This was a grand spectacle for them, and most of them were amazed to see the town bank manager, the last man you'd expect to find holding iron, in this situation.

'Put the gun down now,' Johnny said and the bank manager caught his eye.

He seemed uncertain of himself and for a moment Johnny thought he was going to comply.

Suddenly a man in the gathered crowd shouted to the bank manager and it was the last utterance the man ever made. The shout startled the bank manager and he turned quickly, fired, hitting the man straight between the eyes, pulping his head and sending a burst of blood into the air. It would have been a tremendously skilled shot had it been intentional, but the bank manager had fired without aiming.

Several screams sounded out as the dead man fell backwards into the crowd, and Cherry took the opportunity to drive an elbow back into Carver's stomach. Her blow winded the man but he recovered quickly and dragged her forcefully back towards the bank.

'Don't anyone else move,' Carver yelled. 'I'm warning you.'

Johnny, the kid and the sheriff were on the street, and they each stood perfectly still, none of them raising their weapons. The situation had now worsened and for the moment the only way to keep Cherry Mewis alive was to comply with Carver's demands.

'I want a couple of horses,' the bank manager yelled. 'Miss Mewis and me are going to wait in the bank. Bring the horses and we'll ride out of town. Don't nobody follow me and I'll let the woman ride back when I've covered a goodly distance.'

The bank manager continued stepping backwards, all the while keeping his gun tight against his hostage's head. They finally reached the bank and he spun Cherry around so she was in front of him. He pushed his gun into her back.

'Don't move,' he warned her, as he reached into his pocket with his free hand and took out the bank key, which he placed into one of Cherry's hands. 'Open the door.' He pushed the gun harder into the woman's back.

A moment later and they had both stepped into the bank, closing and locking the door behind them.

'I'm gonna kill that son of a bitch,' Johnny said.

★   ★   ★

Thirty minutes had gone by since Carver had entered the bank with his hostage; the dead had been removed from the street, the crowds dispersed and only Johnny and the sheriff remained. The town's people were not far away, though, and many of them watched the scene from the boardwalk outside the Indian Creek. The kid, leading two horses that had been saddled, came from the direction of the livery stable and when the sheriff saw him he turned to the bank.

'Carver, we've got your horses,' he yelled.

Carver's face appeared in one of the windows. He didn't open the window but used the butt of his pistol to smash the glass. The sounds caused the horses to grow skittish and it was all the kid could do to keep them under control.

'Tether them outside,' he yelled. 'And then you men drop your weapons on the ground and get back over by the saloon. We'll come out when I decide it's safe to do so.'

'Do as he says,' the sheriff said and released his own gun belt, dropping it to the ground as the kid led the horses to the bank and tied their reins to the hitching post. The kid then undid his own gun belt, allowed it to fall to the ground and stepped back to stand beside Johnny and the lawman.

'You too,' Carver said, directing the command at Johnny, who had yet to remove his own guns.

Johnny did so but snarled: 'You hurt that woman and I'll do worse than kill you.'

'Go to the saloon,' Carver shouted. His voice now sounded calm, as if he had accepted his situation and was in full control.

'We're going,' the lawman said. 'You have my word we won't follow but you keep yours and let the woman go.'

'You have my word,' Carver retorted.

What good is the word of a thief and killer, Johnny thought but said nothing.

'Get moving,' Carver commanded and watched as the men walked back down the street towards the saloon. Only when they had stepped up on to the boardwalk did he disappear from the window.

A moment or so later Cherry Mewis let out a scream that could be heard clean down the street.

20

The scream took the bank manager by surprise and he turned back to the woman, confused.

Cherry grabbed an oil lamp from the counter and swung it at Carver. It struck him a glancing blow on the forehead and caused him to stumble, but once again he recovered quickly and lunged towards her. She threw the oil lamp but it missed the man and smashed against the far wall. The sound behind him startled him and, thinking someone was trying to force their way into the bank, he turned and fired. The bullet struck a desk and deflected itself towards the wall with a spark that ignited the oil that had seeped on to the floor. Flames licked at the oil and then chugged like a train along the gelatinous track of oil and spread up the wall.

Carver only paid the flames momentary attention before moving quickly towards the woman and slapped her a stinging blow across the face.

'You try anything else and I'll kill you,' he warned.

*   *   *

'What are you doing?' the sheriff yelled, horrified at the sight of the town bank. The front of the building was now almost completely engulfed in flames. The kid was marshalling the crowds to get buckets, pans, hats even, anything that could be used to carry water and get the fire under control. Not only was the bank manager trapped inside the bank but the woman was in there too.

'He wants a horse,' Johnny said, securing his gun belt tightly around his waist. 'I'll give him a horse.' The sheriff's horse was tethered outside his office and Johnny ran to it. He pulled himself up into the saddle and spurred the terrified horse forward, towards the inferno that had been the town bank.

'Get back here,' the sheriff yelled but if Johnny heard him, which was doubtful since he was currently halfway along the street and moving at speed, then he ignored him.

Johnny had to fight with the horse as he approached the blazing building. The heat was now incredible and the horse tried to buck the rider from its back, but Johnny held tight to the reins, spurred the horse even harder. The bank was now directly in front of him. Johnny removed his bandanna and, fighting to keep the horse under control, he placed it over the beast's eyes, using it as a blindfold. This momentarily confused the horse and Johnny urged it forward, sending it directly into the door of the bank. The wood splintered and Johnny jumped from the horse and allowed it to run back off down the street, the bandanna falling from the creature's eyes. The two horses the kid had tied to the hitching post outside the bank were also going frantic and Johnny quickly untied them, gave each of them a slap on the rump and sent them galloping off away from the tremendous heat the burning bank was giving off.

Johnny kicked at the door and it gave, flying open.

He then cleared leather and went into the blazing building.

It was hell in there.

Johnny had to shield his mouth with an arm as he swallowed a lungful of the acrid smoke. For a moment he buckled over as he coughed but he recovered quickly, wiped spittle from his lips.

'Carver,' he yelled. 'Cherry.'

There was no answer, not that Johnny would have been able to hear any response above the roar of the flames. The fire had spread towards the bank counter and the flames were making short work of the thin wood, which acted as a protective barrier between the bank tellers and the customers.

Johnny took a look behind him. There was still a way out through the ruined front door, but it was only a matter of time before the fire spread and made escape impossible.

'Cherry,' Johnny yelled and once again doubled over into a coughing fit. He knew he had to find them.

Find them pretty damn quickly.

He couldn't remain there much longer before the smoke and heat overpowered him. The fire had gained dominance and even now the flames were growing higher and would soon cut off any avenue of escape.

Had Carver gotten out somehow?

Left the bank by a rear exit and, unseen, made good his escape?

Johnny shielded his eyes and peered around the bank, but the visibility was poor. The smoke was so thick that it was like looking through a shroud and all Johnny could make out were indistinct shapes. The flames cast a hellish glow over everything and the smoke was growing ever thicker.

'Carver,' Johnny shouted again and this time he was answered by gunfire as a bullet tore into the wall behind him.

Johnny crouched down, his own weapon ready for the first sight of a target.

'Cherry,' Johnny yelled.

Crouching, Johnny was below the worst of the smoke and he saw something ahead of him, an unidentifiable shape. At first he wasn't sure if it was Carver or Cherry but then he realized it was Cherry Mewis.

She was lying perfectly still on the floor, maybe six feet away from him.

'No,' Johnny screamed. Don't let her be dead. Oh God please don't let her be dead.

Another shot sounded, coming from his left and Johnny fired back in the general direction.

On all fours he scrambled towards the woman. He reached her and pushed her gently but she didn't respond, didn't move at all. There was a thin trickle of blood on her forehead as if she had been struck a blow.

Johnny reached out for her throat

and felt for a pulse, but for a moment there was nothing and once again he felt a terrible wave of anguish overcome him. In a fury he fired off two shots into the smoke, firing in the direction the earlier shots had come from.

'Carver,' he screamed. 'You son of a bitch.'

His gunfire was returned, two shots, both bullets missing their target and striking the walls with a burst of sparks.

Johnny once again fired back.

It was then that Cherry moved, coughed.

Johnny looked down and she opened her eyes.

Thank God, he thought. Oh thank the Lord. She's alive. He pressed his face in close to hers and asked her if she could get up, walk.

'I think so,' Cherry managed. Her eyes widened in terror as she saw the blazing inferno around them. She clung tightly to one of Johnny's arms.

'On three,' Johnny said, 'I want you to get up and run for the door. Don't look back until you feel the fresh air.' He pointed in the direction of the door. 'Shield your face the best you can, keep your head down and run. Do you think you can do that?'

She nodded.

'Good,' Johnny said and reached out and with a thumb he smeared the blood on her forehead and saw the tiny wound. He realized that it was nothing serious but that was the least of their concerns in any case.

Unless they got out of there immediately nothing would ever matter again.

'You ready?' he asked.

Cherry nodded, coughed.

'One,' Johnny said and slid an arm behind her, helping her until she was sitting upright.

'Two.' He helped her up, got up with her. They were now both standing and he looked at her, nodded in encouragement.

'Three. Go!' He pushed Cherry forward and she started running but Carver, unseen amongst the fire, saw her move and fired at her. Thankfully he missed but Johnny had seen the flash of his gun and he fired back — once, twice, thrice and then he heard Carver scream out in pain.

Johnny wasn't sure if he'd killed Carver or not but he wasn't going to wait around to find out.

Let him burn, he thought.

Carver's fate no longer seemed important and Johnny had more pressing concerns. The fire was now beyond control, and would soon completely devour the building and all those within.

'Keep running,' he shouted and ran at speed towards the door.

He caught up with Cherry and grabbed her tightly around the waist, almost taking her off her feet.

Together they shielded their eyes and ran through a blanket of flames before coming out into the mercifully cool air.

At the very moment that Johnny and Cherry emerged from the inferno someone threw a bucket of water.

It shocked both of them as it sloshed against them.

Nothing had ever felt so good, so refreshing, as that bucket full of cold water.

Johnny collapsed, coughing, to his knees, and beside him Cherry did pretty much the same but also vomited into the dirt.

Johnny smiled and looked at her. She was now kneeling beside him, panting in chunks of the clean air. A lot of her hair had been burnt and her face was covered in a thick sheen of black. There were clean-looking smears around her eyes and mouth and speckles of vomit upon her chin.

At that particular moment Johnny thought she had never looked quite so beautiful.

21

'A fine job,' Johnny said and slapped the kid upon the back. 'A damn fine job.'

'Yep,' the kid agreed. 'We've got some pretty good horse flesh in there.'

'We'll make our fortune yet,' Johnny laughed and pulled his makings from his shirt. He quickly put together a quirly and handed the makings to the kid.

'Is that beef I smell?' the kid asked and placed his own quirly between his teeth. He took one of the Lucifers from the box offered by Johnny and struck it against a boot heel.

'I guess so,' Johnny said and felt his own stomach rumble. Sweet potatoes would accompany the meat, which would be topped off with the most delicious gravy imaginable.

'Sounds good,' the kid said.

'Come on.' Johnny placed an arm around the kid's shoulder. 'Best not keep Mrs Jerusalem waiting too long.'

Mrs Jerusalem. Johnny felt immense pride each and every time he said it. It had been more than six months since he and Cherry Mewis had stood together in the town church, and made the vows that had joined them together for the rest of their lives.

We do hope that you have enjoyed reading this large print book.

Did you know that all of our titles are available for purchase?

We publish a wide range of high quality large print books including:
Romances, Mysteries, Classics
General Fiction
Non Fiction and Westerns

Special interest titles available in large print are:
The Little Oxford Dictionary
Music Book, Song Book
Hymn Book, Service Book

Also available from us courtesy of Oxford University Press:
Young Readers' Dictionary
(large print edition)
Young Readers' Thesaurus
(large print edition)

For further information or a free brochure, please contact us at:
Ulverscroft Large Print Books Ltd.,
The Green, Bradgate Road, Anstey,
Leicester, LE7 7FU, England.
Tel: (00 44) **0116 236 4325**
Fax: (00 44) **0116 234 0205**

WYOMING BLOOD FEUD

Dale Graham

Neither Rafe Charnley nor his son Jeff could have foreseen how quickly their family tensions would escalate when Jeff falls in love with the daughter of the sheepherders with whom the family have a long-standing feud. Rafe cannot see his son's actions as anything but a deeply personal betrayal. Jeff is desperate to prove his feelings to his father — but when his beau's brother is accused of violating a land boundary, Rafe threatens to have him strung up. Can the hostilities between them be rectified without blood being spilled?

McGRAW RETURNS

J. W. Throgmorton

Twenty years in prison tamed Jack McGraw, or so he thought. He returns to Crockett, Texas, where he meets his daughter, Rebecca, for the first time, and discovers that he must save her and their farm from Ben Page. Unknown to Rebecca, Page has found crude oil on an unused part of the farm. A sample sent to Pittsburg confirmed its value, and Page alone knows it's worth millions. He sends his henchmen to kidnap Rebecca, and soon McGraw finds himself on a three-state rescue mission . . .